MAXTON

LAUREN TYLER

For Larry

PROLOGUE
2019

He took the coward's way out, which could also be the stubborn male route. He didn't call anyone. He didn't tell anyone he was coming home. He just showed up in the same fashion as when he left.

It had been four months, one week, three days, and maybe four hours since he saw his family. That was one month, one week, three days, and four hours longer than planned.

His pain was manageable, and the rest of his recovery would be better handled surrounded by familiar faces instead of a foreign hospital. He wouldn't die from his injuries flying first class on a twelve-hour international flight home. Especially if he drugged himself and slept the whole way.

Now here he was. The crossroad was deciding who to disturb first—his father at the family's main house or his ex-wife and son at the cottage he left them in.

"Take a left here," he told the driver just before the drive split. The left curved into the trees with the appearance of a secret passageway into the woods with no end in sight, until a slight curve opened up to the quaint cottage he called home for the past few years—two thousand square feet of history built at the turn of the century by his great grandfather for the hired help. The white siding was dusky in the moonlight, the gray trim badly in need of touch-ups, but the lanterns burned bright along the driveway leading to the front porch. She left the porch lights on, the late spring breeze causing the flag in front to sway casually, not a care in the world. He noticed all the things he never noticed before—flower pots, porch rockers, the lion-shaped door knocker, a yellow welcome mat that said HELLO, and four pairs of rain boots in gray, blue, pink, and yellow, large, medium, and two smalls.

Refusing help, he took his two bags and a backpack and surveyed the house. Unable to avoid stepping on the chalk art, he slowly walked up each step until he reached the land-ing, slightly winded. Open the door or knock? Open or knock?

He really hated himself right then.

He set the bags down and gripped the knocker, banging three times before letting it drop and stepping back. Silence. What if she was working? What if no one was home? What time was it? Were they sleeping?

He looked to his right wondering if he should just grab his bags and trek it to the main house. He might even be able to sneak inside without anyone noticing, crawl into bed, sleep for a week, and then face the music.

Too late for that though as the door swung open. He could not stop the smile from spreading across his face. *He was a grown ass man, and he refused to cry. Her tears would not bring his own.*

"MAX!" the teenage voice yelled before gangly arms threw themselves around his neck. He could feel her tears soaking into his now moist t-shirt. The guilt of leaving his sisters, his child, and the woman he loved was almost more painful than the physical razor blades that filled his body when she squeezed around his chest.

"JULES! BB!" she called after a moment, her hold loosening and allowing him a moment to breathe deeper.

And now he was deaf as she yelled back into the house. He kissed her temple, wrapped an arm around her, and just let her be, let her soak it in, his eyes clenched shut. Rani—his not so little sister—had grown in the past year and looked more adult than awkward teen.

It was a singular word that wrapped around his heart and squeezed, the one that finally brought the first tear cascading down his cheek.

"DADDY!" Baer screamed before jumping in one bound into Max's free arm, nearly causing his pain and weakened body to stagger under the force. He clenched his eyes shut and sucked in a shaky breath. He never let himself imagine the feeling of his son pressed against his chest.

Then, tiny arms wrapped around his legs, and when he opened his eyes, Brinkley and her head of blonde curls were holding on for dear life. Jules was leaning against the doorframe watching him, her own eyes filled with tears.

Hi, he mouthed to Jules.

Hi, she mouthed back. She let him soak it in for a few minutes before breaking the silence. "Okay, guys. Let's let Prince Charming into the house." She rubbed Rani's back briefly. "Grab a bag."

Rani let go of Max hesitantly, afraid he would disappear. She took the hand of her little sister, who was wrapped around Max's ankles, and picked up one of his bags before heading through the front door.

Baer was enforcing his five-year-old choke hold with brute force, refusing to let go. "He's okay," Max whispered to

Jules, keeping hold of him and reaching out his free hand to her. "Come here."

He took Jules' hand and pulled her to his side, wrapping an arm around her just like he had Rani. He kissed her forehead when she buried her face in his neck. On the outside they would look like the American Dream. Jules brushed away a tear and looked up at him.

In that moment, nothing felt more right than being with them and being with her. Kissing her felt like coming home. It was simple and easy, and for a split second it made him forget everything. Forget they were no longer married. Forget the shooting in Africa. Forget why he ran away from home.

"God, I missed you," he whispered against her lips as he pulled back.

"Come inside."

She stepped away from him and picked up the last two bags before walking inside. He followed her. After much protest, she managed to get the kids into bed and found him sitting on the floor in the den with his back to the couch, head back, eyes closed. The twinkling sound of ice cubes brought his eyes open as Jules held out a glass with golden liquid. He took it from her, and they clinked their glasses together.

"There are more comfortable spots than the floor," she whispered. He attempted to smile, but it never reached his eyes. Everything felt like it took more effort than it should.

"I've slept in far worse."

She sat down next to him, and they both sipped from their glasses.

"You really scared me," she told him.

"I'm sorry. If it's any consolation, I scared myself."

"Tell me what happened." She was given the bare minimum of information before this moment. He was shot, he was recovering, he was coming home. She wanted to hear from him what he experienced.

He sighed, and without a second thought, finished off the liquid in his glass. He held it out to her like a kid asking for more milk. He would need more alcohol if he was going to revisit his introduction to death. He knew he probably shouldn't be drinking with the kinds of painkillers jetting through his system. His head had yet to stop pounding. But he didn't really care at the moment, and Jules wasn't arguing with him.

He took a deep breath, knowing he needed to be honest with her. Where did he even start? "It's a little blurry. I might have pissed off the wrong army. Or maybe I helped the wrong one." He took a sip. "It was my last night at the camp. In the morning we were going to drive back to the capital for a night before my flight the next day."

"We?"

"Doctors from the camp." He avoided it. At least he was good at that. "There had been a lot of fighting and so far, we had been lucky to avoid getting in the middle of the politics. We were treating a gunshot victim, not very successfully, when we were ambushed. Ended up right between the two opposing sides. I was trying to save this kid who was probably fifteen, and they were screaming at me to stop."

"Why didn't you stop?"

"Because I'm a doctor." It was a simple answer, and it was also a stupid one. A stupid decision. But could he have lived with himself if he stood back and let someone die, especially a kid?

"They made an example out of me. Two shots," he said, touching his shoulder and side. "They had me on my knees with a gun to my head while the director tried to negotiate. I don't speak the language. I have no idea what he said. One guy hit me with the butt of his gun. Then they took a couple turns kicking me." He took a small drink. "I blacked out. When I woke up, I was in an actual hospital bed."

"Hudson, you could have died. You didn't even call me. She called me." Jules remembered the first phone call from Africa. Carrie worked with Max, that's what she told Jules when she called and broke the news that Max had been injured and was being transferred somewhere in Europe.

The second call was from his doctor, but he didn't share a lot of specifics. When Max finally called, he was checking out against medical advice and was coming home to her. To them. She was a walking anxiety attack for almost two weeks waiting for him to get home.

"There's nothing you could have done," he told her. "Not from so far away."

"I could have flown there and helped out." She watched him, waiting to see if he would keep talking. "You were alone in a different country. I can't even imagine what you were feeling or thinking with no one to talk to."

"I'm here now. That's all that matters."

"It's really hard not to hate you right now," she told him. She never thought it was possible to hate and love someone at the same time and both with the same passion.

"I don't blame you." Sip. "I'll make a full recovery, and then you can beat the shit out of me if it makes you feel better."

"Don't tempt me." She waited a beat, took a sip from her own glass. "So, where are you now with said recovery?"

"Just waiting for the pain to go away. I'll probably need some scans before I go back to work. Get the stitches out."

"Work? Are you sure you want to go back so soon?" The idea of letting him out of her sight again made Jules' stomach turn.

He shrugged. "I'm not talking about going back tomorrow. Pain management first."

"And where does it hurt?" she asked, putting on her doctor's hat.

"Everywhere," he said honestly. "But each day it gets a little better." He didn't want her to keep worrying. He just wanted to do anything he could to get them back to normal. Whatever that was.

She rested her head on his shoulder then immediately turned and looked at him, laying a hand on his forehead.

"You're burning up." It was more than pain, more than a couple gunshot wounds. He was at risk to have picked up a number of major viruses not prevalent in the U.S.

"Just a virus. I'm on antibiotics."

"Yeah, right. Come on. You're going to bed."

"With you?" He smiled.

"No funny business." She helped him stand and took his now empty glass, setting it down on the coffee table. He leaned on her, just to feel her body next to his after so long, the familiar curve of her hips, the hands he'd watched heal and soothe. All he wanted was to let her take care of him.

1

———

ONE MONTH LATER

"What are you doing?" Max asked, trying not to look into the mirror above the fireplace.

"Stop moving," Rani told him in mock anger, grabbing his chin with her scrawny fingers and making him face her.

"It's almost eight. Did you finish your homework?"

"Four hours ago."

"This is so cool," Rani's best friend, Jessica, said, coming into the room and into Max's peripheral view.

"Rani, you better not make me regret this," he threatened.

"Trust me. It's so cool. And it's just one TikTok."

"I would prefer not to be in any TikTok."

"All the kids are doing it."

"I'm not a kid."

"Yes, you are," she told him, wiser in her sixteen years than his thirty-six.

"Thanks."

He didn't know how he got into this precarious position. The only excuses that came to mind were medical house arrest and some bored teenagers in desperate need of enter-tainment.

A month ago, he was in the middle of the African jungle with Doctors Without Borders, twenty-four hours from his flight back home, when their vehicle was ambushed coming back to the capital from a small clinic. He was trying to save a young gunshot victim and ended up one himself. If he was being honest, most of the details were fuzzy, but the pain was very real.

Now he was home recovering from two bullet wounds, a severe concussion, and a hairline fracture to his sternum. Tomorrow he would go back to work as an emergency room senior attending on light duty.

"Are you almost done?" he asked, adjusting to relieve any amount of pain in the uncomfortable chair.

"If you'd stop moving, we would be done already," she told him.

The doorbell rang. He looked at his watch and felt a wet lick swipe under his eye and across his cheek.

"Damn it," she cursed.

"Language!"

"I'll fix it, you get the door," Jessica said.

"Rani," he growled.

"I promise, PC." She grinned at him and his scowl over her shoulder then bounded out of the room on unicorn-socked feet.

"Don't call me that," he yelled after her with lack of effort. *Prince Charming*. That's what all her friends called him, even in ear shot.

She slid the last few feet to the front door, almost sliding past it, before grabbing the handle, twisting, and pulling it open.

Laughing in the way only a sixteen-year-old girl could

without anyone comprehending the meaning, she grinned at the platinum blonde guest waiting on the other side.

"Hi," Rani said, her giggle subsiding.

"Hi," the visitor said, suddenly nervous, second guessing a surprise appearance. She couldn't help taking a small step back to make sure she was at the right home. The same black Range Rover was in the circular drive. The address was the same one written on a scrap of paper. She was at the right house. "Is Max here?"

"Yeah," Rani said, still smiling. "Come in. I'll go get him."

She didn't think twice before making the same bumbling and sliding path back toward the den, skidding almost past the entry before calling out.

"PC, your girlfriend is here!"

The guest looked around with a smirk. How do things change so much and yet not change at all? The entry still looked the same. Same furniture and painting above the entry table, similar size twelve tennis shoes, leather jacket on the hook, backpack lopsided against the wall. Throw in a teenage girl, tiny shoes belonging to tiny humans, matchbox cars, and a unicorn headband, and she could tell the years had passed and some things had definitely changed.

Max stuck a finger in the abandoned beer bottle on the end table once he removed himself from the clutches of two teenage girls and headed for the front door.

"Clean up this mess," he called to them before taking a long drink, thinking maybe work would be a more welcome treat than being confined to a home with teenagers and children all day long. No one had been to visit since he got home, and what little effort he was using to scroll through the list of possible visitors, the one he encountered wasn't even in the running.

He stopped suddenly at the woman in the entry. Long,

stick straight platinum blonde hair, form fitting low rise jeans, happy yellow sweater that seemed to laugh in his face.

"Dani," he said, reigning in the prepubescent crack at the blast from the past standing in his entry. She spun around with a smile then, without even thinking, started laughing.

Of course he knew what he looked like. In reality, this was not the first time he let his baby sister dress him up for her entertainment. He was a picture-perfect emo punk rocker with black eyeliner, growing beard, and mini man bun. He had debated cutting his hair but then saw that it kind of went with his new brooding demeanor, and he didn't want to ruin his reputation.

"I'm not sure if I should be insulted or flattered," he said casually. It wasn't just the makeup and general lack of personal care; he had just spent almost a year in a country where showers, deodorant, and personal hygiene were the last thoughts.

"She calls you PC?" she questioned.

"Don't get me started."

"I'm sure it's good. How the mighty have fallen," she told him, trying to suppress a laugh.

"I'm not sure what to say," he said with a raised eyebrow.

"PC!" a voice called from beyond.

"That's not Rani, is it?" she asked.

"In the flesh."

"Last time I saw her she was wishing for her two front teeth and asking for a pony for Christmas."

"She got the pony."

"Incoming!" a bite-sized voice yelled with expert preci-sion. Max shot out his left arm and grabbed the propelling five-year-old before he collided with a wall or family heirloom as the scooter that was under him slowed to a stop almost immediately bumping the leg of an end table.

Max sucked in a deep breath, gritted his teeth, and fake swooped the child toward the ground before hanging him over his shoulder. He glanced at the grandfather clock in the hall.

"It's 8:30. PJs, teeth, etc."

"Daddy," his whine muffled.

"Where is Brinkley?" Max asked, setting the boy down.

"Library."

"Okay. Upstairs. Now."

The boy scrambled toward the stairs, and with a very typical five-year-old howl, called out. "BRINKLEY. BEDTIME."

Max stood and watched the child grin at him before scrambling out of sight upstairs.

"PC!" Rani called again.

He gritted his teeth and mockingly growled under his breath. "I need to go," he said, taking another look at the clock. His phone started ringing from his pocket. Probably the evening FaceTime call with Jules.

"I should have called." She hadn't expected to arrive at a house with so much activity. The Max Hudson she remembered worked and slept. He didn't live in the family mansion, he didn't have children, and he didn't wear eyeliner.

He laughed softly and shook his head. "Honestly, I probably wouldn't have answered." He knew it was kind of harsh but so was her disappearing act eight years ago. "I don't answer unknown numbers," he said trying to sound less like the asshole he had turned into.

She tried to keep a brave front. She knew it wouldn't be that easy to just show back up in his life—a life he'd obviously moved on from without one thought about her.

She tried to smile, letting his insult slide. "I'm going to go."

Max shook his head but didn't get to voice an objection or agreement before the little patter of feet echoed through the halls and down the stairs, appearing at his side.

"Did Mom call?" the boy asked.

Max fished his phone out of his pocket, still looking at Dani, and handed it to his son. The little patter echoed back as he retreated out of the room.

"Why did you come here?" Max asked her, stuffing his hands into his pockets. He was all seriousness now, coated in makeup, and she smiled softly at him.

"I didn't think you knew, and I didn't want you to just show up and find out."

"I have no idea what you're talking about. I'm a little bit out of the loop as of late. Didn't know what?"

"Kids and all," she offered as an excuse.

"Right," he said, letting her assume kids were the reason for everything. His blue eyes stared at her. He didn't feel like hashing out the last month or his reason for being clueless as to why she was suddenly showing up at his house.

"I'm back in the ER. Pediatrics. First day was about a month ago. I was surprised to find you weren't there. Overheard you were coming back tomorrow and just figured..." she trailed off.

He stared at her. "Oh," he said, before reaching for his beer and taking a drink.

"I just didn't want it to be weird. I thought you should hear it from me."

"Thanks," he said, but didn't move from his spot. "Then I guess I'll see you tomorrow."

"Maxton, stop making out with your girlfriend and get back in here," Rani called from the other room. *Maxton* was code that Rani meant business.

"I really have to go," he said, glancing over his shoulder.

"It's my music video debut, and the natives are getting restless," he said casually.

"I can tell. See you tomorrow."

"Sure." The coward in him wanted to call and beg his boss for a few extra days off, but he knew he couldn't avoid Dani forever. The "Mad Max" in him wanted to push Dani away, run her out of town, and repress the anger he still felt over her leaving him the first time. He wasn't sure he was strong enough to let her back into his good graces.

Dani looked curiously at him for a second before turning and opening the door. With one more glance over her shoulder at him, she walked out. He didn't hesitate before walking back into the den to his sister and her best friend.

"That was rude," he said.

"So is keeping us waiting. Who was that?" Rani asked.

"Dani." He assumed Rani probably had vague memories of Dani, but that was a long time ago. He didn't expect her to remember some fleeting girl in his life from when she was a child.

"Are you guys getting back together?" He guessed wrong.

"We were never together to begin with."

"That's not what Jules says." He rolled his eyes.

"Shut up and do this video," he said knowing this would turn him into a hospital joke but would also win him the Best Big Brother in the World award.

"Daddy," Baer said ten minutes later, walking into the room in his Lego pajamas, followed closely by Brinkley in her pink princess dress.

Max was sitting on the couch being tortured watching their Tik Tok video on repeat. He motioned them over, and both kids climbed into his lap, handing his phone back. The best part of the day. The silence and the snuggles he missed out on over the past year.

"What'd Mom say?" he asked.

"Sleep tight, don't let the bed bugs bite," both kids said with yawns.

He scowled when Rani posed next to them for a selfie, and within seconds his phone pinged from the tag of her Instagram. *Happy little family time.*

"Okay, bedtime." He got up off the couch in one swoop, holding a sleepy five-year-old in each arm. "I'm back at work early tomorrow. Rani, you're on deck. All the numbers are in the hall just in case. Jules will come by before she heads to work."

"I know," she said.

"Don't stay up too late. Rosie will be here around nine. Try to do some school work." He was so glad to come home and find Rosie still employed by his father. She was a life saver with cooking, cleaning, babysitting—basically all the things Max sucked at. She practically raised him, why not help raise his son and sisters.

"Yes, Dad," she joked.

He disappeared out of the room and instantly heard the giggles and chatter that can only come from teenage girls. Maybe the fact that she was his sister was the reason it didn't grate on his nerves constantly. Or maybe it was refreshing to be around kids whose biggest worries were grades, zits, and if the cute boy in English noticed their new jeans at lunch.

It wasn't disease or famine or death.

An hour later, he walked back downstairs and through the silent house, turning off lights and checking for locked doors. He saw teenage painted toes poking out of a makeshift fort in the den and heard the soft but heavy breathing of exhausted adolescence.

He kept a lamp on but killed the rest of the lights and the TV. Slowly the house slid into darkness. He checked the locks one last time and was walking back upstairs to his room when his phone started ringing.

Jules checking up on them. They may no longer be married, they may still have a complicated relationship, but there was comfort in letting her take care of him, knowing someone had his back, someone he could trust with his life and his family without question.

"Hi," he said quietly before closing his bedroom door.

"How'd it go?"

"Took four stories and thirty minutes of back rubs."

"That kid takes after you with his insomnia."

"He could have inherited worse traits."

"Are you ready for tomorrow?"

"Sure."

"Liar."

He took a deep breath and let it out slowly.

"What?" she asked. She knew that sigh. He wanted to protect her feelings, not his own. He could hear the sound of machine beeps, rolling wheels, overheard pages, the never-ending noise that comes from working in an emergency room.

"Nothing."

"Liar." She waited to see if he would fess up. "Is it the pain? Because you don't have to start back tomorrow. You're not even fully healed. Your scans still showed a hairline fracture."

"Did you know Dani was back?" he asked, ripping off the band-aid. He was lying down on top of the covers of his king-sized, four-poster bed that was built for royalty. The ceiling fan spun above him, reminding him of the first hospital he woke up in, opening his eyes to see it spinning in the humid heat, doing little to cool them down. Heat was the least of his problems then. The pain set in almost instantly, and the fan became something he could concentrate on.

"Why didn't you tell me?" he asked finally, breaking himself out of the memory when Jules remained quiet.

"Because I didn't want to add one more thing to everything." It was his turn not to respond.

"I should have told you." The background noise faded, and he could picture her walking into an empty exam room or the lounge for privacy, so no one would hear her talking.

"She came by the house to tell me. How did she even know where to find me?"

Last time he saw Dani, he had been living in a rental on the opposite side of town from his family. She'd only been to the family house a few times for events as his *female colleague* and *friend*.

"I'm sorry." This was Jules' version of a confession, and he knew she probably helped facilitate the reunion.

"It's fine. I guess it's better to know than be surprised tomorrow."

The sound picked back up, and he heard elevated voices.

"I have to go. Try to get some sleep. I'll see you in the afternoon when I'm back on shift."

"Bye," he said into the moonlit room and the silent phone.

2

THE NEXT DAY

"Hey, I thought it was just a rumor," Marco said, coming out of the elevator to fall into step with Max. He held out his hand and the two shook.

"Never believe any rumors about me," he grinned. "I thought you already knew that."

They were instant friends when they met five years ago, the two lone men on a tropical beach vacation with their significant others. But they had a rocky start to their professional relationship when it came to patient care as the top surgeon and the ER doc. Marco was probably the only male friend he had that was worth any effort, and his best friend after Jules. They were at the same trust level, except he had no desire to see Marco naked, and luckily Marco had no desire to see Jules naked. Win win.

"Of course. When did you get back?" Marco asked, bringing him back to the present.

"I flew into Boise a few weeks ago. Had a little recuperating to do. First day back to work."

"Make up for lost time?" Marco said with an eyebrow raise.

Max laughed. "Maybe a little."

"Aren't you guys divorced?"

"Technically."

"That usually means you stop sleeping with her."

"Why give up a good thing? It's not like we're seeing anyone else." Max gave him a satisfied grin. "Give me the news. What have I missed out on?"

"Aside from the usual corporate BS, not much."

"Who are you seeing this week?"

"Cute candy striper up in pedes." Max knew he was lying, but this is what they did.

"A teenager?"

"She's twenty-seven."

"Likely story."

"You have no room to judge, sleeping with your ex-wife. Are you back for good?"

"Yeah. If it wasn't for almost dying, the bugs and heat alone would have me running back sooner rather than later. Plus, I need to be here for Baer. I worked out my issues. Back to new," he said, trying to convince himself more than anyone else.

"Worked out your issues, huh? What was her name?" he asked, not even attempting to hide his smile.

"It is frightening how good you are at that."

"I did a couple years in psych along with surgery." They walked into the lounge, and Max poured two cups of coffee. "What was her name?"

"Carrie. It wasn't anything serious."

"Local? Foreign? I want all the details."

"You will not get all the details. She's from Texas. Been working a rotation in Sydney. Her next stop was New York.

We worked in the camp together. Fiery red hair. Fiery red temper."

"And she was totally cool with you coming home." Max shrugged as they walked back out. "Did you even tell her?"

"I was unconscious," he defended, holding out his hands.

"We have two rolling in ten minutes out. We'll need you, too, Marco," Alex said.

"So, you just left."

"Shitty phone and internet service. I was in Paris. She was in Africa. What was I supposed to do?" Max asked.

"Oh, man. I'll pray for you and your karma." Max laughed. "You meet the new pedes attending?" Marco asked eying Dani coming their way from an exam room.

"Yep." Max watched her for a second before taking a drink of his coffee and grabbing the gloves thrust into his hands. He turned and found Marco looking at him, arms crossed. Apparently, he was o and 3 for hiding all his dirty little secrets today. "What?"

"This is so good. It's better than any daytime TV."

"Shut up," he said, setting down his coffee cup.

"So, let me get this straight. Jules, Meg, and now Dani, all under the same hospital roof. And Carrie," he drew out with exaggerated slowness.

"I never claimed to be smart. Or classy."

"But you can certainly pick them."

"Dani was just a friend."

"With benefits? Like Jules?" Marco said, hearing the siren approach.

"Nothing like Jules."

"Hudson and Marco, take number one. Dani, grab number two," Maine said, appearing out of nowhere.

"Like you wouldn't marry her?" Marco asked over the

patient as orders were called and they pulled into the trauma room.

"Like I don't want to have this conversation right now," Max said, listening to the airway. All conversation dropped, aside from patient care. Max focused on the last six months of ride or die decisions in Africa to pull him through, never second guessing and praising God for the resources available at his fingertips.

"I think we have a hip dislocation."

"Is he out?" Max asked. It would be painful, and their patient would definitely react if he wasn't sedated.

"Like a light."

Marco walked a first-year resident through stabilizing the patient as Max braced himself on the top of the gurney.

"Don't tell Jules about this," Max said with a smile. Famous last words.

Dani and Maine both turned at the loud crash next door. "Go see what happened," Maine told an intern who scrambled to the door only to come back a second later.

"Dr. Hudson's on the ground. I don't think he's awake."

"Damn it," Maine said. "Dani, keep working." She pushed open the door between their rooms where the intern was kneeling over Max. "What the hell happened?" She knelt down next to Max; his eyes wide open.

"Fell off the gurney."

"What was he doing on the gurney?" She felt for a pulse at his neck and suddenly Max gasped.

"Dislocation," Marco said. "Patient is stable now."

"Great. Max, don't move. Where does it hurt?" she asked.

He glanced over at her. "You're kidding, right?"

"Fine. Get me a backboard and neck brace."

"No. Just give me a second to breathe."

"How about some morphine?"

"How about a shot of Jack?" He smiled at her.

"Smart ass. Alright. Let's get you up." Marco came over and the two of them helped him stand. He instantly doubled over, leaning against the counter. "Marco, take your patient up. Max, next door."

He hesitated a second then brushed off her arm and led the way to the exam room. She pointed to the gurney, and he sat down.

"I had big plans to just leave you alone and not ask about your limitations, but it looks like that's out of the question now."

"I just got the wind knocked out of me."

"I want to know every single piece of you that hurts and where you are injured," she said before putting a stethoscope to his heart and listening.

"Maine," he said. "You received a copy of my file."

"I don't care. I want to hear it from you." He just looked at her. This sucked. "What?"

"Do a sternum x-ray. Just in case. Don't tell Jules." She gave him a hard look then nodded.

"For now."

3

SAME DAY

"What are you doing?" Jules asked, walking into the lounge hours later to find Max laying on the couch holding a chart over his face, his left-handed scrawl filling the lines, and a coffee cup sitting on his chest.

"Charting."

"Lying down?"

He glanced over at her as she headed for the coffee maker. He gave a low tsk and when she turned, he was holding out his coffee cup.

"Lazy." He just winked as she walked over with the pot and refilled the cup.

He watched her putter around the lounge and felt a wave of warmth spread over him. Could he even remember the moment when he looked at Jules and his thoughts changed from "this is my best friend" to "I want to see this woman naked"? Yes, he could. But it still felt like a dream sometimes.

She made the most mundane thing look sexy, like pulling her dirty blonde hair up into a messy bun or opening the fridge out of boredom and not finding any food. Her fingernails were midnight blue, her eyes grey pools, and when she bit down on her lower lip in contemplation before closing the fridge door, he nearly groaned remembering two nights ago when she did the same thing in a different setting.

"You're staring," she told him, and he blinked quickly, clearing his thoughts. She smirked. He looked away.

"When did you get in?" he asked.

"Couple hours ago. Had a meeting. Someone had to pick up the slack while Mad Max was away."

"Just when you think you're on the easy train," he said, taking a sip of his coffee before setting the cup gingerly on his flat abdomen and going back to writing.

"Seriously, why are you lying down to chart?"

"I'm icing my back."

"Still in pain?"

"I'm pretty sure pain is my new middle name. I'm beginning to think it will never go away."

"Did you take something?" she asked, opening her locker.

"Not yet." She shook the over-the-counter pill bottle at him, and he nodded. Such a mom. She placed four tablets in his open palm, and before she could get away, he pulled her palm to his lips and kissed it.

He was a sucker, and he was quickly realizing how much he missed her. It was so easy with Jules.

The door to the lounge swung open, and Bobby, one of the third-year residents, came bounding in covered in blood, followed by Kelley, his partner in crime.

"Dude, can I get your autograph?" he asked, opening his locker and coming out with a new shirt.

"Why?" Max asked.

"Because you're the latest rock sensation."

"What are you talking about?" Max asked.

"TikTok," Bobby said.

"Is that why you're wearing eyeliner?" Jules asked, looking at him curiously. She noticed something was different, but for the life of her, she hadn't been able to figure it out. Between the mop of dark hair and the beard, his crystal blue eyes had darkened.

Could have also just been the pain.

"I'm not wearing eyeliner," he said as the lounge door opened again. He should have scrubbed his face harder.

Bobby was down to just a pair of slacks and no shirt. They all made quite the demonstration of hospital professionalism at the moment.

Dr. Maine, Chief of Emergency Medicine, walked in wearing her best suit, followed by Dr. Dani Wendell. "Dr. Johnson, why don't you have a shirt on?"

"Trauma 1 had a gusher all over my shirt."

"That's what bathrooms are for. Dr. Max Hudson," Dr. Maine introduced. "You know Dr. Dani Wendell, new pedes attending."

"Welcome back," Max said without looking away from his chart, thinking the couch would make him disappear.

"Same to you," Dani said with a slight nod.

"Do you need to go home?" Maine asked Max.

"No," he said behind the chart.

"Are you icing?" she asked.

"Second pack."

"Pain killers?"

"Yes."

"Good. Next time don't be a hero. Save that for Africa," she said. Max lowered his chart and looked at her. She raised an eyebrow his way. She did it on purpose. *Thank you, Dr. Maine.*

"What did you do?" Jules asked, looking at him.

"Patient vs. Doctor. Round one. I lost," he said casually before looking back at his chart.

"I have meetings for the rest of the day. Hudson, you take the lead until the end of your shift. I'll be back. Don't teach Dani any of your bad habits," Maine said.

"Of course," he said with a smile, and she grunted an approval before turning to leave the room.

"Teacher's pet," Jules said.

"Jealous," he retorted, looking at her.

"Patient vs. Doctor?" Jules questioned after a moment of silence, pulling the chart out of his hands. He instinctively grabbed the cup of coffee before it spilled and burned his skin.

"We were trying to set a hip dislocation, and the patient didn't like it. Next thing I know, I'm on the ground."

"Kicked off the gurney?"

"Not the first time. Won't be the last."

"Did you get checked?"

"I'm fine," he said before sitting up with a wince.

"What hurts?" she asked.

"Back off, Jules," he said in all seriousness. They weren't going to play this game at work and definitely not with Dani around. Dani took that time to skate past them to her locker, key in her code, and swing it open.

Jules felt the shift. There had been subtle signs of his mood swings, but nothing so quick as this moment. *Mad Max.*

"I'm serious about the autograph," Bobby said.

"Get out," Max told him. Bobby pulled the new shirt over his head and walked out with Kelley hot on his heels.

"Don't pull the asshole routine," Jules told him, handing him back his chart. She didn't care if anyone heard her.

"Can we save this for later?" he asked, glancing at Dani.

"Don't mind me. I could use a little entertainment in my life," Dani said, slipping into her white coat and closing the locker. "Kind of miss the bantering. My old hospital was pretty boring."

"I mind," Max said, not looking away from Jules, reaching for the door to storm out in his perfect male temper tantrum fashion.

"Jules, incoming," a nurse said, pushing open the lounge door at the same time, hitting Max perfectly in the middle of the chest before he could move.

"Shit," he growled, grasping his chest, nearly dropping his coffee as he sucked in a breath.

"Are you okay?" Jules asked, rushing over to him and placing a hand on his shoulder. He brushed her off.

"I'm fine. Just go," he told her with a wave. She only hesitated a second before walking out of the room to greet the incoming trauma.

Max grabbed the discarded ice pack and pressed it to his sternum, waiting for the wave of nausea and pain to pass.

"Just another day in paradise?" Dani asked from her leaning position against the lockers.

"Yeah, I guess so," he said sarcastically. His pager started going off. This day already sucked. He looked around the room to make sure he had everything, and with the ice pack still pressed to his chest, finally looked at her.

"Are you okay?"

"No," he told her honestly. His pager went off again. "Let's go," he told her before pushing open the door with an elbow and holding it open for her.

4

SAME DAY

Finally, that's all he could think. Finally, this day was over. Finally, he could go home. Finally, it would no longer be his first day back at work. Finally, people would stop asking if he was okay or stop giving him looks. Finally, he didn't have to see Dani walking in the halls and keep wondering about the past.

With a quick glance over his shoulder, he grabbed a fresh long-sleeve shirt, stripped off his soiled scrub top, and was pulling the new one over his head when the door swung open. He couldn't help a quick look over his shoulder in panic and breathed a sigh of relief. He didn't need everyone seeing the healing damage to his body.

"Almost caught you," Jules said. He half smiled over his shoulder. "I barely saw you all afternoon."

"I know. It was crazy."

"How are you feeling?"

"Better." He closed his locker and turned to her. "And that's the last time I'm answering that question for the foreseeable future."

"I only ask because I care."

"Thank you, but you can care in other ways." He turned to her, closing his locker, and slowly smiled.

She raised an eyebrow at him. "Really?" *Prince Charming.*

He took a step closer. "They say endorphins are great for the healing process." Another step.

"They?" she didn't move, just watched him advance, like a lion stalking his prey.

"Helps with bad moods, sleepless nights, instant pain killer." They were toe to toe, and he had that naughty glint in his eye, trying not to grin, daring her to do anything. "Just what the doctor ordered."

"Not this doctor."

He tilted his head to the side slightly and brushed the escaped beach waves from her bun off her neck, slowly dragging one finger from her ear and down to her collarbone.

"You still have eyeliner on." Her comment made him smile, and he leaned down slightly until they were almost nose to nose, eyes locked.

"You used to have a thing for 80s rockers and man buns," he told her, despite the fact he had his dark mop of hair perfectly ravaged in place. He was half a second from kissing her when Maine pushed through the lounge door with Dani, both of them halting as if they just walked in on a very compromising position.

Max grinned without an ounce of guilt or shame at Jules before stepping back arms open in an *I give up* gesture. He walked over to the coffee machine and grabbed a to-go cup.

"How was your first day back?" Maine said, nudging Max from his spot blocking the coffee pot. "Did you get checked out?" she asked him casually.

"I'm a doctor. I checked myself out," he said. "Got a gold

star and a lollipop." Maine looked past him to Jules who just shook her head. Max's phone rang, and he fished it out of his pocket.

"Yep," he said with a quick answer. "I'm about to leave. Pizza?" he questioned.

"No," Jules said, interrupting him.

"What?" he asked her innocently, covering the phone. It's possible he had been serving pizza or leftovers to his son and sisters for at least a week. He turned his back on Jules. "You want the usual?" he asked into the phone.

"Where's Rosie?" Jules asked him, reaching for the phone. He batted her hand away.

I'm on the phone, he mouthed to her. She may be the mother of his child, but she was not his wife anymore. He was capable of handling dinner.

"Working," Max told Jules before going back to the phone. Even listening to a teenager and Jules, he somehow picked up on the silent conversation between Maine and Dani.

"Who's all there? I don't want to feed the neighborhood," Max said into the phone.

"They have to be sick of pizza," Jules told him, trying to take the phone out of his hand again. He used his forearm to playfully hold her away from him.

"There's a boy at my house," he nearly yelled into the phone and rolled his eyes at Jules. "Fine. Jessica can stay for dinner."

Jules spun out of his way and expertly managed to take the phone out of his hand pulling it up to her ear. "No pizza. Pull the chicken out of the freezer and set the table. I'll be there in twenty minutes, and I'll cook you real food." She hung up the phone and handed it back to him.

"I didn't invite you over, and aren't you still working?" he said, putting his phone back in his pocket and taking a sip of his coffee. While he primarily occupied and owned the main house now that he was recovered and they were divorced, she still lived within walking distance. To any outsider they would still look like a traditional married couple. Coming over uninvited, regular family dinners, carpool, and even sleepovers.

"Half shift and standing invitation. Are you coming?" she asked him, heading for the door.

"Not yet," he said with a devilish grin and a wink.

"Fine." She grabbed her bag and left the lounge. "I'll see you at home."

"See everyone tomorrow," Maine said before closing her own locker and following Jules' lead. "Hudson, this was not light duty. No traumas tomorrow. No heavy lifting. More teaching."

"Scout's honor," he said, holding up three fingers.

"Go home and ice your back."

He was about to hit her with another sarcastic retort but took a sip of his coffee instead at the look in her eye. Dani looked over at him as she shrugged into her light jacket and closed her locker. Maine left them alone in silence.

"Africa, huh?" she said.

"Yep."

"How long?"

"I forget." He held her gaze. "Why are you back?"

"I forget," she countered.

"Touché."

"Still playing by your own rules, I see."

He was torn between spilling all the secrets of the past few years to her, but also keeping them under lock and key. She left him, or rather she left the state, without a glance back. She left without giving them a chance to become something. She left before he could ask her the one question he ended up asking someone else.

"How's the family fortune?" she quizzed.

"Locked up tight and safe from the gold diggers and thieves."

"How long are we going to dance around everything?" she asked, crossing her arms. He was good with his one liners and comebacks, deflecting the question, and overall avoidance. That hadn't really changed. She knew she would have to be the one to initiate any real conversation between them.

He finished his coffee and tossed it into the trash. He wanted another cup but would settle for a beer when he got home. "I don't know."

"What's the hold up?"

"I don't know. I need to learn to trust you again," he said carefully. The words dug into her. He saw the hurt cross her face and almost wanted to take it back.

"Nothing has changed for me," she told him honestly.

"Everything has changed for me." His blue eyes reflected emotions she wasn't sure she wanted to know about, and she wondered truly how deep this pain inside him went. When he said he was not okay, it felt like more than a reflection on his physical condition. Had she really hurt him that badly by leaving?

"I see that very clearly. Are you two dating?" she asked.

"Who?" he replied, knowing full well who she was asking about.

"Jules."

"No."

"Looks pretty cozy to me."

"She's my best friend." Dani used to be his best friend.

"That exchange," she said motioning to the middle of the

room where he was previously standing toe to toe silently daring Jules, "was more than friends."

He looked down, his first true sign of weakness and hesitancy. It wasn't some big secret to everyone else, but it would probably be a shock for Dani. When she left, Jules was a co-worker, an acquaintance, nothing more.

"She's my ex-wife," he said with a shrug before pushing off the counter and opening the door and walking out.

5

2014

"She's my wife," Max said, looking at his father.

They hadn't been inside the house for more than thirty minutes, drinks barely poured, before his father started in on him about this, that, and the other thing. The same boring routine that encompassed why Max was still a doctor, why Max wouldn't settle down, and why Max would bring some random woman into their family home for a private family gathering. Thank God his sister was off at some slumber party and didn't have to be subjected to the lecture.

"What?" his father said in shock.

"John, leave him alone," his grandmother said.

"This is supposed to be a family dinner," his father commented. "A private family dinner."

"Jules is family," Max reiterated.

"I know what you are up to," he said, pointing a finger at his son.

"John," his father's new, much younger wife, Justine, cautioned with a gentle pat on his arm. Max's stepmom could easily be his own new wife.

"I'm just saying it's a little convenient."

"You are not saying anything else on the subject. My life, my wife. We can leave if it's that big of a deal," Max told him, setting his glass down and reaching for Jules' wine glass, fully intent on leaving.

"You are not going anywhere," his grandmother said. "Why don't you tell us the story of how this all came to be," she suggested, taking a proper seat on the couch.

Max looked at Jules. She smiled and shrugged. This was his show.

ALL JULES WANTED WAS SOME QUALITY GIRL TIME, DRINKS by the pool, a little flirting with some locals at the clubs, and sleeping in until noon. They would read books and gossip and have absolutely no agenda, there wouldn't be blood and guts and vomit everywhere she looked.

Then one girlfriend canceled. The second decided to invite her boyfriend. The third found out she was pregnant, and baby daddy came to make sure she was safe.

Bags packed and waiting for her car to arrive for the airport, Jules was torn. This was not the trip she had planned. She was working on her first pre-vacation mimosa when her phone buzzed.

MAX: Is it okay to think of you naked every day you're gone?

JULES: Ha ha.

MAX: I'm serious. Send photos. Send nudes. That's better.

She stared at the phone in her hand then the clock. There was a very small window of opportunity to adjust the plans. This was either a brilliant idea or the stupidest idea.

JULES: Why don't you just come with me?

MAX: *Now who's joking?*

JULES: *I'm serious.*

The little bubbles popped up; her foot started taping. This was a stupid idea. A horn honked outside—her ride. She downed the rest of her drink, pocketed her phone, and grabbed the suitcase and carry-on. Max would never be able to get the time off work. With one of them gone, that meant he was already working extra to pick up the slack.

She wanted to make sure she was plenty early to the airport for an obligatory airport bar cocktail. There was still no response as she cruised through check-in and TSA pre-check.

"You are just in time to order," Jacque, her BFF who now came with a boyfriend, said when Jules walked up.

"Good. Make it a double."

"What's wrong?"

"Nothing. Just had a lapse in judgement. I'm so ready for a vacation."

Their drinks arrived, and she took a long sip.

"What kind of lapse in judgement?" Marco, the boyfriend, asked.

"The very spontaneous invitation for someone else to join our trip."

"Who? Is this the mystery man you won't tell anyone about?" Jacque questioned.

"I don't have a mystery man."

"Yes, you do. Who else are you always busy with?"

"It's called work."

"Not at midnight."

"Sometimes we go get drinks after our shift."

"We?"

"Max," she said matter of fact. They knew Max. He was her resident wingman. It was believable that she would spend time with him outside of work. What they didn't know up

until this point was that Max had also turned into her resident friend-with-benefits.

"Speaking of," Jacque said, nodding behind them.

No time like the present.

"Fancy seeing you here," Jacque said as Max approached their table and rested his hands on the back of Jules' chair tilting it down a bit.

"I called Maine. Then I called in a few favors." He was speaking to Jules as he reached over to shake Marco's hand then fist bumped with Jacque.

"Okay," Jules said softly.

"The only seat I could get was first class."

Jacque looked at Jules, her lips forming a small O before sliding into a smirk.

"Okay," she said.

"So, I bumped you up with me so I wouldn't get lonely," he smiled.

Jules turned and looked at him. "What?"

"There she is," he said with a grin before leaning down and kissing her, then with dramatic flair he tipped her chair back more for a moment before setting her upright and pulling out the chair next to her. "What are we drinking?"

"You said you went on vacation with a friend," his father said.

"I did," Max told him. "A girlfriend."

"How do you go from a girlfriend to a wife in ten days without your family even knowing you had a girlfriend."

"John," his stepmom said. "Max is a grown adult. He does not need to introduce all his girlfriends to his overprotective father."

"*I would certainly think if marriage were on the table, he would be splashing her around.*"

"*Splashing? More like hiding. You like them more my age than your own,*" Max told him, refilling his glass. "*No offense,*" he said to his stepmom. She just smiled at him.

"*Were you already engaged? Was this planned?*" his father asked.

"*No and no.*"

"*Maybe a little,*" Jules corrected him with a wink. "*We talked about marriage a little bit.*" Just not in the way his father was implying.

"I HAVE A PROPOSITION FOR YOU," MAX SAID, HIS EYES covered in dark shades as they lay by the pool two days later.

"*You've had quite a few of those lately,*" she joked.

"*Not that kind. But now that you bring it up...*" he lowered his glasses and looked over at her.

"*What's your proposition? I don't feel like doing anything else but this right now.*"

He was silent. She looked up from her book when he didn't respond. His glasses were back on, and he was just lying there.

"Hudson," she said. He smiled. He hadn't been Hudson in a while. They were the Starsky and Hutch of the ER. It was a running joke that where one was, the other could be found close by. They had built-in GPS. In years to come, she would be known as Hudson's Jules. She was his crown jewels, she was the keeper of the family jewels, or whatever smartass remark they could come up with.

"*What do you think about marrying me?*" he asked. He didn't want to look at her face. He didn't want to see her reaction. He didn't want to feel torn open or weak. He was always *the guy that everyone thought had it together—the money, the girls, the grades, the career.*

"What are you talking about?" she asked, sitting up to face him. He didn't move.

"Marry me."

"Is this another one of your practical jokes?"

"You know I don't joke. Definitely not about relationships."

"You know I love you, but it's not like we're actually in a 'relationship'," she told him using air quotes. He glanced sideways at her. She finally reached over and took off his sunglasses, so he was forced to look at her.

"How more compatible do we need to be? We already spend most of our time together, I've already seen you naked, and I really like that part, we have known each other for years."

"You're on the rebound."

"No, I'm not," he said unconvincingly.

"I'm on the rebound."

"That guy was an asshole." He smiled at her. "I'm an asshole."

"No, you're not."

"D*ID YOU TAKE A RING*? D*O YOU EVEN HAVE A RING*?" *HIS dad asked, trying to look at Jules' hand that was holding her wine.*

"We're doctors. Rings are kind of an issue," Max said.

"You didn't even get her a ring?"

"I have a ring," Jules said, pulling a chain from under her shirt and holding up the ring hanging from the end.

"Maxton," his grandmother said softly, instantly recognizing her old engagement ring. She had given it to him years

ago, around the time he was pining after Dani. Max kneeled at his grandmother's feet as she took his face in her hands.

"You told me to save it for someone special, someone who was worth it. Jules is worth it. It's not a ploy, it's not to cheat the system, it's not for any reason other than Jules makes me happy."

"If she makes you happy, then I'm happy," his grandmother kissed his cheek and squeezed his hand.

"Is she pregnant?" his dad asked. At that Jules finished her glass of wine and set the glass on the coffee table. Max was at his limit, too.

"Grami, I love you, but we're leaving," he kissed her cheek and stood.

"I'll see you next week," she said softly.

Max took Jules' hand and nearly dragged her out of the room before there were any more protests or comments.

"Well, that was fun," she said.

"I feel like it's just the beginning. He's not going to make this easy on me."

It was a moment he would never live down. He stole his father's thunder. Max Hudson getting married would always trump John Hudson's pending announcement that his new, younger wife, Justine, was expecting a baby.

6

PRESENT DAY (2019)

"I feel like I'm starting at square one. A whole new beginning," Max said to her lying back on the floor.

Thing 1 and Thing 2 were finally fast asleep in his bed after many arguments and debates. Rani was confined to her room finishing an essay and not allowed to come back out until morning. They were alone at the main house like so many times before, and yet even voicing those words, he wasn't just talking about work. He felt like he was starting over with Jules, if that was even possible.

They hadn't had much alone time since he came home. Between the kids and doctors and now work, finding some silence was hard to come by. Silence with Jules was easy. They didn't require conversation.

Africa was silent when it wasn't chaos. He liked the silence.

"This is how it all started," she told him with a smile.

"How what started?" he asked.

"How we started."

She was curled up in a chair under a blanket looking

down on his worn face as he lay sprawled on the rug in front of the fireplace. She remembered all their moments like these over the years - as friends and as lovers. Before kids, hiding from the kids, hiding from themselves, before there were problems, before divorce, before he left.

"No, it's not," he countered.

"Were you hit in the head in Africa?" She waved off the question instantly knowing, of course, that he still was recovering from a concussion.

"Pretty sure I remember how it started."

"It started in the bar. We just lost that family of three in a really bad car accident. You refused to let me just go home, better to drink together."

"What are you talking about?" she asked. "That was months before."

He looked over at her. "Before what?"

"YOU, ME, THREE BOTTLES OF WINE ON THIS FLOOR IN front of that fireplace." He smiled at her like he had a dirty little secret.

"Yeah, that wasn't the beginning."

"Pretty sure I didn't sleep with you before that day."

"Since when does sex qualify as the beginning?"

"It's a pretty definitive beginning. Until you sleep with someone you don't really ever know if it's going to work out."

"I had a pretty good idea."

"Hudson, may I remind you that only a few months before that you were in a relationship with another woman."

"What can I say, when I know, I know."

"You knew, when you were dating Meg, that you and I would end up where we are today?"

"Well, it wasn't that specific. And I wasn't dating Meg. I was sleeping with her."

"Same thing."

"No, it's not." He sounded like so many typical males afraid of commitment, assuming a casual relationship with someone when the other party was most likely thinking the exact opposite.

"Did Meg know this?"

"Yes, unfortunately, I am the asshole who did that to Meg."

"That night in the bar, didn't you guys just break up?"

"Yeah."

"In the middle of a trauma, right?"

"I am not proud of that moment. Just another reason you wouldn't let me go home alone."

"I had a blind date. I needed a wingman to rescue me if it went bad."

"Which it did." He smiled.

"Which it did," she repeated. "Still have no idea how that rates as the beginning of our torrid love affair."

"It wasn't torrid."

"You're changing the subject."

"There's nothing to say."

"I want to know why you feel that was the start of 'us.'"

"Agree to disagree. Maybe it wasn't for you, but it was for me."

"How?"

"Can we just drop it?"

"Definitely not."

He was silent, staring at the ceiling. Jules let him lay in silence, just watching him, and waiting. She refused to let this drop. This was obviously something important in Max's version of events, and that meant it was important to her.

"Stop staring at me," he said finally, and she smiled behind her wine glass.

"How long are you going to torture yourself?" Jules asked as she leaned over to refill his wine glass and hers.

"Don't start in on me," he said with his eyes closed.

"Are you just punishing yourself? Because I'm pretty sure you've met the quota of penance for a lifetime."

"I'm kicking you out if you keep talking about this."

"No, you won't."

He sat up and leaned against the coffee table, taking a sip of his wine before looking at her. "How am I torturing myself?" he asked, giving her a tired look. He shifted, winced, and pressed a hand to his side.

"Why won't you just tell me what was so significant about that night?"

"It's not significant to you so it doesn't matter."

"You matter to me."

"It was a long time ago."

"Who cares. I thought we didn't keep secrets."

"It's not a secret."

"Are you embarrassed? If it's not a secret, there should be no problem telling me."

He looked over at her. She wanted him to show his hand, but it's not like it would change anything, so what was the point? Why tell her that he thinks the moment he fell in love with her was at a bar while he watched her make small talk with a stranger, only hours after he publicly 'broke up' with someone else?

When she flicked her hair over her shoulder and pulled on her ear, it was a sign for him to save her.

The feel of his hand around her waist and his lips on her cheek to make the stranger back off was the most feeling he'd had since Dani left.

When she asked him to dance, her fingers twisted in his hair.

As she hailed a cab and rested her head on his shoulder and fell asleep.

As he carried her inside his house and tucked her in a spare bedroom fully clothed.

"Okay, fine. We can talk about something else." She looked down at him.

"Anything else," he said, shaking off the memories he kept hidden from that night.

"Dani. She went out of her way to come here to see you. Don't shut her out." She ignored the roll of his eyes and the pained look he shot her way. It was cheating a bit to shift from one topic he didn't want to discuss to the other topic he had been avoiding. Was the look he gave her annoyance or displeasure that maybe she was trying to get him to move on with someone else? "A lot has happened since she left."

"And a lot more can happen now that she's back."

"Maybe I don't want her anymore."

"Bullshit." Was it really bullshit? Was it a line, or was it the truth? He sighed, and she just watched him.

Deep down he was still the man Jules met over ten years ago. The first time he winked at her over a patient, she had butterflies for days. He had her back when she was blamed for a patient death that wasn't her fault. He rescued her from sleazy pick-up lines at bars and held her when she cried at a failed long-distance relationship.

He could flirt one second and throw a punch the next, whatever was needed in the moment. He could be passionate to a fault, but when it came to matters of the heart, he usually lacked the self-confidence to make a decision.

Did he do the same thing with Dani? With Meg? Was

she just another notch in his bedpost in the search for happiness?

"Can we just let the cards play out?" He turned his head and looked at her. It was that look. He was changing the subject.

"Don't look at me like that."

"Remind me again why we got divorced." The corner of his mouth twitched slightly.

"Because we're not in love with each other. We played it safe."

"Says who? What's so wrong with safe?"

"You were never one to play it safe."

"I learned the hard way that maybe safe is the way to go."

"Do not let what happened in Africa force you to play it safe."

He held her stare. Was that what was happening? Did Africa change him, or did divorce change him? Maybe he should have gone to therapy years ago. Or even when he got back. Work through all the childhood trauma, his mother's death, his father's abandonment, the bad breakups.

"I'm going home," she said, not moving from her comfortable spot.

"You can stay," he said casually before setting down his wine glass and standing up. He held a hand out to her, and she took it.

"I'm going home," she confirmed, slipping her feet into her shoes.

"My shift starts at nine." He followed her lead to the front door. Adjusting their schedules for the kids was a fun adventure in adulting. It was hard to track who was where and when. A shared family calendar alerted them constantly and kept Rani in the loop of where she could find her guardians at any given moment.

"I'm off. I'll be here by eight." He held out her jacket, and she slipped her arms in. She turned to him as he adjusted the collar. "Can you make sure that Rani does her homework before anyone comes over?"

"It's not my first rodeo," she said softly, looking at him. He looked exhausted and five years older than he really was. "Are you sleeping at all?" she asked, resting a hand on his arm.

"You can stay and read me a bedtime story," he whispered, taking a step toward her, forcing her to step back. He stepped again and took her hand, interlocking their fingers.

"Hudson," she warned. The wood of the front door stopped her from moving away from him. She knew that look in his eye. She'd already given in to that look multiple times since he got home, and almost daily while they dated and were married. She needed to stop letting that look change her mind, letting his blue eyes hypnotize her.

He didn't give her another chance to weakly protest before he kissed her. Trapping their entwined hands above her head, he snaked his free hand in her coat and pulled their bodies flush against each other.

"What are you doing?" she whispered.

"Shut up," he said before deepening their kiss. All it took was a little nip on her bottom lip for her to grant him access. His tongue swirled with hers, and her soft moan made him deepen further. Her free hand tangled in his already messy locks, while her other squeezed his where it was trapped.

Kissing Max Hudson was like the first scoop out of the peanut butter jar—creamy, fresh, smooth.

Sometimes it was never-ending. Sometimes it was trouble. Like now.

She didn't register that they had been interrupted until someone coughed loudly.

Max, never one to show embarrassment or shy away, kept his hands on her but let go of her lips and without looking away nearly growled, "What Rani?"

"When you're done making out with your *EX-wife*, can you read over my essay?" she asked.

"Yes," he said. "I'll be up in a minute." He could see her out of the corner of his eye just standing there. "Go away now," he hissed.

Rani smiled before uncrossing her arms and heading back upstairs.

"I'm going home now. For reals," Jules said, putting a hand to his chest. He reluctantly took a step back and released her other hand.

"Party pooper," he said.

"You are trouble," she told him.

"You've never complained before."

"I'm not complaining now. But I am going home. See you in the morning."

She pulled open the front door and closed it without another look. He locked it after her then let his head drop to the wood with a thud.

He was an idiot.

Finally, he pushed away from the door and started up the stairs.

"Ready?" Max asked, stopping at Rani's open doorway. She was lying on her stomach with her laptop open in front of her.

"Sure," she said, sitting up criss-cross. He sat down on the bed next to her, and she handed him the laptop. He started reading, knowing full well she was staring at him. "What?" he asked, without glancing up.

"Are you getting back together with Jules?" He froze.

With a deep breath he sat back against her pillows taking the laptop with him.

"No. I don't know." He gave her a sad smile. He didn't even know the right answer—how was he supposed to set a good example for his sister when he could barely control his own teenage-style urges that further complicated a relationship that ended over a year ago.

"Then why were you kissing her?"

"Because I'm an idiot." When he married Jules, Rani was living with his father full time, and Max rarely saw her. They didn't become closer until Baer and Brinkley were born, and even more so after Justine was diagnosed with breast cancer that took her life. Max became a constant refuge for his teenage sister.

"Do you still love her?"

"I will always love her. Jules is my best friend and Baer's mom."

"Then why didn't you guys just stay married?"

"I asked her the same thing tonight. It's complicated, and I'm sure you'll understand better when you're older." She looked at him expecting more of an answer. "We're not in love with each other."

"How do you know? Is there really a difference?"

"For some people." How was it that his sixteen-year-old sister was the one trying to rationalize his behavior and question his feelings? He did love Jules. But for them, was it any different than being in love? What kind of love was theirs?

"Are you in love with someone else?" she asked innocently.

"I don't know."

"Is it because of Dani?"

"What do you know about Dani?" He glared at her with a mock pout. Apparently, she was more observant than he gave her credit for. "I don't think we should be talking about my dating life. We are supposed to be working on your essay."

"So, you are dating Dani."

"I am not dating anyone. If I was dating someone, I would not be kissing Jules."

"Good. Because that would be a pretty douchebag move to kiss a girl you're not dating behind the back of the girl you are dating."

"You are correct. And I don't want to be the resident douchebag."

"I liked Dani," she said once they had drifted back to silence, and he was reading her essay again. "And I love Jules."

"Drop it," he said.

"Do you not like Dani anymore?"

"I don't like you right now," he joked, gently shoving her with his foot. He gave her a quick glance before going back to the computer.

He heard her tapping away on her phone and hoped that was the end of the conversation. Ten minutes later, she was back to staring at him.

"What now?"

"Are you done yet?" she asked.

"Yes. It's good. I highlighted some areas and made notes. Jules will be here in the morning if you want her to give it a final read before you submit it."

"Thanks!" She took the laptop back as he got off the bed then leaned down and kissed the top of her head.

"Don't stay up too late."

"Promise."

He walked out of her room, closed the door part way, glanced into his bedroom where the mini terrorists were taking up every inch of space in the king-sized bed. With a sigh he headed back for the stairs and went back to the den. The fire was still blazing.

Pouring a refill in his wine glass, he lay down on the couch as his phone buzzed; a handful of notifications popped up on his Instagram feed. *What had Rani posted now?*

He had a new follower. Clicking on the username, Dani's face and profile popped up.

7

ONE DAY AFTER AFRICA (2019)

Max wasn't sure if he was more miserable back home from Africa or in the hospital, but he knew it was going to be a day of pain the moment his eyes opened. He felt like he was still sleeping under a mosquito net based on how his clothes stuck to his body and the sweat dripped from his forehead. It might as well be 110 degrees in Boise.

The room was still dark and a quick look at the clock showed it was already 8 a.m. He wasn't sure how much sleep he got but knew it wasn't enough. He missed the days of drug-induced nights that provided no nightmares, and he woke up numb.

He could be weak when he was alone, but he needed to get control when he was around other people. He slowly got out of bed and with a silent prayer and gritted teeth managed to get through a shower that left him feeling more refreshed and clean.

Slipping on a pair of black joggers and a t-shirt, he found a pair of his slippers in the closet and walked out of the room and down stairs. He could hear the morning chatter he missed so much with little kids, the early morning cartoons, and plastic plates. Africa was gunshots, hushed whispers, crying.

"Is there coffee?" he asked, walking into the living room where Jules was leaning against the doorframe watching the kids stare at the TV.

"Hey," she said. "I'll get it for you."

"It's okay. I don't need you to do everything for me."

"Didn't seem that way last night." She helped him undress, gave him a sponge bath, played mother and doctor taking his vitals, hooked him to a saline drip, coaxed him to sip some soup, and finally tucked him into bed. She fell asleep next to him an hour later when her worry turned to exhaustion.

"Jet lag."

"Is that why you hardly slept?"

"Sure," he said before walking into the kitchen. He was taking his first sip of real, fresh coffee when she placed a hand on his forehead.

"You're still warm."

"It will go away in a couple days, I'm sure."

"I was just going to make up some breakfast if you're hungry. Then I was thinking maybe Rosie could watch the kids."

"Why don't we just go next door? Rosie can cook. It looks nice outside. The kids can play," he suggested, leaning against the counter.

"When did you talk to your dad last?"

"I don't remember. Before he left for New York." He thought for a minute, between the concussion, pain killers, and no sleep, trying to pinpoint a memory was not the easiest. "Five months ago?"

"So, he doesn't know you're back."

"No. Why?" he asked. She half shrugged. "He said he would be gone for a couple weeks and you were taking care of everyone. I just assumed he was back." He looked at her. She was hiding something. "Why are Rani and Brinkley sleeping here?"

"Just a slumber party."

"Jules, I know when you're lying, and I definitely know when something else is going on."

"I offered to help out. It was getting overwhelming for your dad."

"Taking care of his own kids is overwhelming?"

"Baer is used to being with Brinkley all the time, and I couldn't just leave Rani in that house alone."

"With her father. Right?" He let the silence continue. "He came back, right?"

"Hudson."

She only used Hudson for three reasons—she was mad, trying to make a point, or she had a naughty look in her eye.

"Let's go over there, and I'll talk to him." He set his coffee cup down, prepared to march over and clear the air with his dad.

"He's not there."

"Where the hell is he?" he asked.

"New York, I think."

"Still? Did he come back at all? And don't even think about lying for him, Jules."

"How about you keep me out of this, and you call and talk to him yourself?"

"You're in this as much as you don't want to be. You married me. You divorced me. You're the mother of my son. You've apparently been taking care of my sisters for months."

"Don't be mad at me. I've done all of this for you, our son, and your sisters."

"I don't want to fight with you," he said defeated, laying a hand over his chest. "Let's just go to the main house. If anyone deserves a break, it's you."

She sighed and walked off. It had been a long time since they had any sort of argument. It never set well, and when it came to Max, it could take days for it to burn off and things return to normal.

While he finished his coffee, she got everyone out of their pajamas and ushered out the door.

MAX WAITED UNTIL THE KIDS WERE FULLY ENTERTAINED with Rosie, eating Mickey Mouse pancakes for breakfast, and a planned afternoon of fun and games before he disappeared into his father's office. Jules didn't ask, she just followed him, carrying two cups of coffee.

"You don't have to be here," he said before he started to dial his dad's number on the speaker from the desk phone. He wasn't really upset with her, but he was definitely taking it out on her since she was the only adult in front of him.

"I know, but I want to be," she said, handing him a cup. He smiled at her. This wasn't what she signed up for, he knew that. But he also knew she was loyal, and through everything, he could count on her. The family drama that had unfolded from the moment they were married would have been enough to scare anyone away. She stuck by his side even after they separated, eventually divorced, and the past year while he was gone, and remained steady now that he was home.

She didn't run away. Was that true love or true friendship?

"Hello," his dad's baritone said briskly over the other end, bringing Max out of his thoughts.

"Hi Dad," Max said. He stood over the speaker phone, coffee in hand, and stared at the handset wondering what would happen.

"Maxton. Where are you? I've been trying to get a hold of you for months."

"My phone didn't work in Africa."

"You must have finally found a good connection."

"Yeah. Where are you?" There was silence on the other end, and he knew his father was debating how to answer. Truth or lie.

"Just working. What time is it there?"

Max looked at the clock on the wall. "Nine."

"I always thought the time difference was more. Are you just getting ready to go to bed?"

"In the morning, Dad. It's nine a.m. here."

"Tomorrow?" Max sighed and looked at Jules. His dad was really a piece of work right now. *Breathe*, Jules mouthed to him.

"I'm in Boise. I'm not in Africa."

"What?"

"Yeah, Dad. I'm home, and you're not here."

"I had a business trip in New York. We had some issues with an investor I needed to handle personally."

"That's great, Dad. You told me you were leaving for New York months ago. You would only be gone a couple weeks. When are you coming home?"

"I don't know yet." He heard muffled sounds on the other end.

"You just left Rani and Brinkley here."

"With Jules. She is a saint. She offered to help. Plus, Rosie, and everyone at the house. Rani couldn't miss school, and I didn't have anyone to watch Brinkley."

"Jules is not paid to help you. Jules has a very important job as well and a child of her own."

"Well, you're home now..." he trailed off.

"When are you coming home?" Max asked again with a sigh.

"Probably a couple weeks. I need to see how this plays out. It's a really precarious situation with this investor."

"Two weeks."

"Yeah."

Max didn't even want to deal with it anymore. He hung up the phone and then hung his head. He felt Jules move beside him, laying a hand on his arm.

"You're okay. We're going to be okay."

"He makes me so mad."

"I know. But being mad while he is gone is not going to solve anything, it won't bring him back sooner, and it's not good for your sisters."

"I don't deserve you."

"You're right," she said. When he looked up at her, she was smiling. "Let's go check on the kids, then we can go back to the house so you can relax."

"We can relax here. Watch the kids from the deck," he suggested. He missed so much being gone. He just didn't want to disappear again.

"Sounds perfect."

"What time do you have to work?"

"Seven. We have the whole day."

He wrapped an arm around her, pulling her close, his chin resting on the top of her head.

"Thank you," he whispered before kissing her golden locks and releasing her to go in search of the rest of the family.

8

———

PRESENT DAY

"Hey," Dani said, walking into the lounge in the morning to find Max pulling on his white doctor's coat over a plain black t-shirt. It was only his second day back to work, and he was struggling to keep up his tough guy facade. Being on babysitting duty wasn't going to make it any easier.

"Hey," he responded, his locker closing with a thud. "Coffee?" he asked as he pulled a cup from the cupboard for himself.

"Sure."

Ten years ago, they were two peas in a pod, inside jokes, happy hour, lunch breaks. But then she left, and she had been replaced in every way and more by Jules.

After so many years, she really thought that it would be water under the bridge, and while they may not be able to go back to where they left off, at least it wouldn't be one hundred percent starting from the beginning like strangers. He was the one acting like a stranger.

"Still take it black?" he asked.

"Like my soul." He smiled. That was what they always used to say. "Things okay?" she asked him, purposefully open ended.

"Yeah. Things are fine," he told her casually.

"I'm the one who's out of the loop, and I apologize for just kind of springing back into your life with some expectation of normalcy."

"You don't have to apologize. We all change, evolve, have lives. I'm just off my A-game."

"Makes sense. Kids, wife, Africa."

She sounded so sad when she pointed out how drastically his life had changed since she left. He was so desperately trying to find something that resembled normal. He didn't know where Dani fit into all that or if it were even possible. He wasn't even ready to admit his A-game might not have anything to do with her assumptions. It had yet to even occur to him to ask how maybe her life had changed.

He opened his mouth to reply as he handed her the cup of coffee, but he was interrupted by his cell ringing. "Sorry," he said, and she waved him off as he accepted the call.

"Hey, Dad," he said. "Yeah, it's good to hear from you. How's New York?" Max made a talking motion with his hand to Dani and rolled his eyes leaning against the counter. A hand instinctively pressed into his ribs.

He talked to his father while he was in Africa, before he was injured and before he knew when he would be coming home. It was a three-minute phone call after which Max received a formal email with an attached itinerary. His father was going on an extended business trip and didn't want to take Rani and Brinkley out of school. So, he left them with Jules with promises to return soon.

The last time they talked was when Max came home to find his father was still gone. He'd left Jules stranded with three kids for nearly six months. Like father, like son. The conversation hadn't ended well, and Max had ignored all attempts at conversation the past month.

"What do you mean?" he asked, standing up straighter. "I'm not on leave anymore. I went back to work yesterday." Why did it feel like his own father was skipping out on responsibility? He wanted Max to continue taking care of his sisters for an undetermined amount of time. "Jules has to work, too. I'm not asking Rani to be a live-in nanny for her sister and nephew. She has summer school. She's a teenager." He rubbed the back of his neck. "Fine. If you want her to play nanny and you want to pay her, then you better call her. And tell her you have no immediate plans to come home. Fine."

He hung up, squeezing his phone with white knuckles, she was surprised it didn't crumble from the force.

"That didn't sound good," Dani said.

"Sometimes I wonder who the parent is anymore." He'd spent years after the death of his mom, when Rani was still a toddler, trying to get his father's affection and attention. His father only encouraged him to follow in his financial footsteps. As soon as medical school was mentioned, all Max got was a cold shoulder and barely the money for tuition.

The door swung open, and Maine walked in with Dr. Meg Mckay hot on her heels. "We have two en route. Bicycle vs. car. Dani, you take the bike."

"I can handle the car," Max said.

"No, Meg is going to pass off her overnights, and you are going to do rounds with the interns."

"Maine," Max started to argue.

"I told you yesterday. You go easy, or you go home."

"Fine," he said, pulling open the lounge door and walking to the admit desk, completely ignoring Meg.

"I didn't realize you were back." Meg said, watching him carefully, as she approached his side. They hadn't had a conversation in over a year, and she had only heard rumors about the kind of mood he was in.

"Yesterday." Blunt and straight to the point.

"Just like riding a bike." She smiled, and he was polite enough to give it back.

"Skipped the training wheels this time," he looked up to the packed patient board as she grabbed a stack of charts. "Want to tell me what we got?" He finally looked at her, one hand in his pocket, the other holding his coffee cup. She didn't get a chance to respond before Dani walked up.

"Come find me later if you want a meeting of the black souls," Dani told Max as she passed, grabbing a set of gloves to head to the trauma. Back in the day, that was their code for escaping for coffee when they had a particularly shitty shift.

"Dani?" Meg called, seizing the opportunity. See how Max liked this new turn of events.

"Yeah." She turned, and Max couldn't help but notice the difference in the two women from his past. Dani was blonde and taller, Meg was brunette and shorter. He picked the exact opposite for a rebound. Then he chose Jules, who favored Dani even more.

"It's tradition for us to take newcomers out for 'welcome to the madness' drinks. I don't think we've had a chance to do that yet. Jules invited me when I started. Now I'm inviting you."

"You don't want to do that," Max said cautiously to Dani.

"Of course she does," Meg said. "We can go this weekend. My night rotation just ended, and I think Jules has a night off soon, right Max?" She smiled. He didn't answer.

Dani always considered herself to have a sixth sense and a keen intuition about people. Even after years apart, she knew there was more to Max, to his situation, to his marriage, and almost every conversation he had with someone had a mysterious undertone. Like the next line out of his mouth would be completely unexpected as well as jaw dropping.

"Count me in," Dani said.

"Perfect! I'll get you the details later."

Dani made a beeline for the incoming trauma. Max stared down at Meg.

"What?" she asked.

"You're not even going to let her get some time under her belt before you start up with all the shenanigans."

"I remember you used to like said shenanigans. You're not invited anyway. And she's been here a month. Plenty of time."

"What? It's an all-girls club now?"

"No, but it's also not the divorced dads club."

"But divorced moms are okay?"

"Jules is not your typical divorced mom. She was married to you. That doesn't really count."

"Ouch," he said, putting a hand over his heart.

"Take these charts off my hands before you really regret it." Meg thrust the stack at him, finally feeling a little relief at the banter and return of the Max she remembered.

"At your service," he said.

9

2011

"Take these charts off my hands before you really regret it," Jules said, walking up to Max and dropping five patient files onto his already large stack.

"At your service," he growled with a hint of a smirk before she disappeared.

It had been months since Dani left Boise for a better paying job and the opportunity to rekindle an old romance. Months since he practically confessed his secret love for her, nearly begging her to stay for him, their first kiss, their last kiss.

He knew he was getting on all their nerves but frankly he didn't really care. He was allowed his feelings, and he was allowed to act however he wanted. In his eyes, as long as he got the job done and didn't kill anyone, then it was a successful day.

"Can you sign off on these charts so I can go home?" his intern asked, setting ten charts in front of Max on the desk. Bold move.

"You go home when I say you go home," Max said with a glare before going back to his own charts. Without a second *glance, the intern quickly disappeared pretending he actually had something to do.*

"Mad Max appears to be on a rampage today," Jules commented. He didn't respond. "You could choose to be a little nicer."

"I could choose a lot of things. Right now, nice is not one of them."

"Do you have an estimated date and time when this pity party will end?" she asked, stepping closer to him, invading his bubble, in the hopes he would be annoyed just enough to look at her.

He finally set down his pen and turned. "No."

"Does your party feel like it wants to go out for drinks tonight?" She smiled sweetly. Ever since Dani left, Max's friendship with Jules had expanded. Somehow Jules became the one person he could rely on, who put up with his crap, and even made him smile sometimes. Even when he really felt like shit, he could go out with Jules and brood while she got hit on left and right. She was a good wingwoman. And with her by his side, most of the women in the bar would leave him alone.

"Twist my arm," he said. He picked up his pen and grabbed the stack of charts left by his intern. "After I finish all your work, my work, and my lazy intern's work."

"I know you are really enjoying the new Max and all, but seriously, can you at least pretend that you like people."

"I don't have to pretend to like you."

"Well, I'm your best friend. It's a requirement."

"Does that also mean you're buying drinks tonight?" he commented as Maine walked out of the lounge followed by a fresh face. Max took a quick glance at her then went back to the charts. Short, brunette, a little trace of Italian coloring. She was the exact opposite of Dani.

"Oh, good," Maine said, noticing that most everyone was

gathered at the admit desk. On any given day this would piss her off because if there were patients, there was more work to be done, and standing around was a red flag for laziness. "Everyone, this is Dr. Meg Mckay. She's coming from Las Vegas, and she's doing a half shift today to get acquainted before starting full time tomorrow. She'll be picking up the slack from losing Dani."

Meg gave a casual wave as everyone said luke-warm hellos. Maine mentioned "losing Dani" like she died, not that she just left them high and dry. Like his heart.

"You can shadow Hudson," Maine said.

"I have an intern already." The last thing he wanted was to have a shadow whose eyes were already watching him with intrigue.

"She's a resident. And your intern is off the clock. Send him home," she told him. Max didn't respond, closing a chart. He gave a little finger wag to his intern hiding down the hall and held out the stack of charts to him. "See, now you're free."

Maine didn't leave room for another word and stalked off down the hall.

"Roshambo?" Max said, turning to Jules with his fist outstretched. Meg stood awkwardly watching as everyone went back to work, waiting for someone to give her something to do.

"No," Jules said. She was not going to play his childish game or take on the new resident.

"Are you buying tonight?" Max questioned, his hand dropping to his side.

"No. Richest person buys," she said. "And be nice." She turned to Meg with a smile. "His bark is worse than his bite." Meg cautiously smiled back. "Jules," she introduced herself. "Welcome to the madness."

"*How would you know?*" *Max asked with a raised eyebrow.*

"*I've heard the rumors. Drinks on Hudson tonight,*" *Jules said with a bright smile just to annoy him as all heads within earshot turned.*

"*Damn it! Why does he always pay when I have to work?*" *Bobby complained.*

"*Because I don't like you,*" *Max said casually before grabbing a couple charts.* "*Let's go,*" *he said to Meg as he started off down the hall. Meg didn't hesitate and followed right after him.*

"*Grab a chart, sign your name on the board. We have three trauma bays, five private exam rooms, three shared exam rooms, triage for up to ten, and a waiting area that will fit a million. Be assertive, act like you know what you're doing, and you have the answer even if you don't. Look busy even if you're not. Don't sleep with the interns.*" *He stopped and turned to look at her.* "*Good?*"

"*Golden.*"

"*Great.*" *He pushed open a door.* "*Welcome back, Mrs. Barrett. What seems to be the problem today?*"

MAX WAS DONE. HE JUST HADN'T DECIDED IF HE WAS DONE *with the day, the job, or his life. Would he be any happier if he just quit the hospital, put on a suit, and sat in board meetings all day? Would he be more miserable?*

All he's ever wanted was to be a doctor. It was the only thing he succeeded at. Fresh out of high school he was accepted to three top schools for emergency medicine. His father only agreed to help front the tuition if he double majored in finance. His first year in college, his mom died in a car accident leaving his father a grumpy widow and his baby sister, Rani, motherless.

At twenty, he did everything he possibly could for his family—flying home every weekend, increasing his class load so he could graduate early with his finance degree and focus only on medicine. Until his mourning father decided that since the "important" degree was complete, paying for a degree in medicine wasn't necessary.

He's spent over ten years trying to gain his father's approval in some area of his life. No woman is good enough to marry, no amount of volunteering and sitting on a board of directors worked, and even moving home to be at his beck and call was failing. When Dani left, he gave up his apartment and moved back into the family house to help take care of his aging grandmother and growing kid sister.

The clock was ticking on the life he had grown used to living. His father was doling out ultimatums, and his grandmother was starting to agree that he needed to settle down. He was too old to be strutting around a hospital and bars and bringing a new girlfriend home every week.

And now, the one thing Max wanted most—to be a doctor and save lives—was getting on his nerves left and right. His sanctuary was crumbling, and he was blaming the girl who left him behind. "Tag, you're it," Max said, coming out of his own thoughts when Bobby walked up to the admit desk. He thrust three charts at him. "Mrs. Barrett. Mr. Reynolds. And John Doe in Curtain 3."

"You suck, you know that?" Bobby said.

"Hate to break it to you, but I like women," Max said casually, erasing his name from the board, then heading down the hall to the lounge.

"It's your first day. You have to join us for drinks," Max

heard Jules say as he approached the lounge, already shredding his jacket.

"Don't feel obligated to invite the new girl," Meg said. "Besides, I would hate to interrupt date night."

"Date night?" Jules asked.

"With Max. He's your boyfriend, right?"

Jules actually laughed out loud. "No. Max is not my boyfriend. Best friend, annoying little brother, but not my boyfriend. He's kind of getting over someone."

"So, he's not always like that?"

"I wouldn't go that far. Max has an undiagnosed personality disorder—Max, Manbun Max, Mad Max, and Prince Charming." Jules smiled. "I'm kidding about the personality disorder. He's harmless."

"Do not feel obligated to tell the new girl everything," Max commented walking into the room like he'd been there the whole time. He was an asshole, and it earned him a glare from Jules.

"It's tradition. Right, Max?" Jules smiled, the room silent, until he finally looked over at them.

"What?" he asked, opening his locker, playing coy. Jules shook her head.

"To invite the new doctors out for welcome drinks. And Max is buying." Jules was on a roll today.

"You keep saying that like it's actually going to happen," he said. He fumbled around in his locker. Without warning he pulled off his scrub top and tossed it across the room into a bin, then resumed his search.

"Are we going for full indecent exposure or just a teaser?" Jules asked, closing her locker, not missing Meg eyeing Max like he was a piece of cake, and she was the starved child. Jules did give her the open window that Max was single.

"What kind of wingman am I if I show up in a well-worn scrub top?"

"What kind of wingman are you anyway?"

"The kind that pays. Can we leave already?" he asked, closing his own locker, and crossing his arms over his chest. He wanted a drink, and he wanted to forget about today.

"Only if I'm driving. Meg, you want to ride with us?" Jules asked. Max looked at her like she was crazy.

"Sure," Meg said without hesitation and a smile at Max.

Was she playing with him or was she flirting?

Max followed the girls out, their already incessant chatting about work and clothes and best places to eat made him roll his eyes. It would be a long night. But maybe they would both find someone interesting and leave him to drink in peace.

On the other hand, maybe Meg Mckay was exactly what the doctor ordered to help Max recover. Nothing like a good ol' fashioned rebound to lighten up his mood.

Meg glanced over her shoulder at him with a bright smile. His eyebrow raised, the corner of his mouth twitched, and right before he slid on sunglasses, he winked.

10

PRESENT DAY

"What's incoming?" Dani asked, finding Max sitting in scrubs on a bench outside the hospital.

"Overdose, I think." He didn't even bother to look at her.

"Are you on deck?" She pulled a pair of gloves out of her pocket and started pulling them on.

"Not if you want it," he said with a shrug before taking a drink of his lukewarm coffee.

"Everything okay?"

"Yep." Short and curt. Everything was not okay. But he wasn't about to tell her.

"You know I can still spot your bullshit a mile away."

He gave her half a smile. "Most people can." He watched the traffic, waiting to hear sirens. Finally, he met her eyes.

"What do I have to do?"

"For what?" he asked, tossing his coffee cup into the nearby trash with ease.

"To get back into Max Hudson's good graces?"

He sighed and leaned forward, running his hands through his hair. He was exhausted. He should have known it wouldn't be easy. Africa was hard, but it was easy. He just had to show up and not die.

This real-world life was hard.

He stiffened when he felt a hand on his arm give a gentle squeeze. He looked up at her.

"What do I have to do?" she whispered. It was a shock-wave through his system. He could still hear those same words coming out of his mouth ten years ago when she left him.

"What do I have to do?" he nearly yelled, turning around when she grabbed his arm trying to get him to stop, to stay there with her, to forgive her.

"Max," she whispered. "Please."

"Why now?" He turned to her, his words as piercing as his blue eyes.

"I can't turn this down. I can't turn my back. Not right now."

"What about me? What do I have to do to get you to stay?"

He stood before her, as close to begging as he would ever come. He stuffed his hands into his pockets and just looked at her. Was it fear, anger, sadness? What were his eyes telling her, and what was he trying to hide?

"I can't stay," she told him, laying a hand on his arm. "You are my best friend. There is no one like Max Hudson. Just because I'm not here doesn't mean you are any less important."

"You say that now. I know what distance does to people. I've watched it over and over again. This isn't a different hospital. This is a different state. This is a different life."

"This job has been my dream since I was a little girl. If it sucks, I will come back." She smiled at him, hoping he would

return it, forgive her for following a dream and maybe giving up on another one.

"It's not just a job." She was also going to another man. She had tried to explain it to him weeks ago—the ex-fiancé who had suddenly showed back up in her life begging for a second chance. This was before the job offer had come through. Dani had implied her ex had just received a similar offer and made it conditional on her joining his team, moving back to be with him, and start fresh where neither of them had history.

Max turned away from her, dragging his hands through his hair. They never even had a chance to start much less have a second chance. He was too much of a coward, wanted to play it safe, wanted to give her all the time in the world to get to know him, to not be run off by another man forcing himself into her life, or just another man hitting on her good looks.

"Max."

His name coming from her lips was what he fell in love with first. The first time she ever called him Max, not Hudson, not a jerk, or an asshole, or a rich bastard. Just Max.

He spun to look at her, seeing the sadness in her eyes. Or was it pity? He was just some poor sap who fell in love with her. How easy it was for her to start her new life, leaving him behind. They all left him behind.

She held her ground when he took the two steps to close the distance between them. She didn't fight him when he tangled his hands into her hair and kissed her like he'd been dreaming of doing for months, for nearly a year. It only took a second for him to realize she was kissing him back, her hands wrapped in the front of his shirt pulling him closer, not pushing him away.

Freeing one hand he wrapped it around her, pulling her flush against his hard body. Everything was hard, and he knew she could feel it. This was it. This was all he was ever going to get, and it was going to have to be enough.

Their tongues danced. He felt one hand slide under his shirt, nails scraping down his back. He moaned against her lips. From a passerby it would look like two lovers finally reunited. It didn't look like a final goodbye.

Max slid his hands down to her shoulders, her arms, to find her hands. It felt like his heart was going to explode. Slowly he pulled away, stepping back, gripping her hands to release him.

"Goodbye," he whispered before finally breaking all contact and without another word turned and walked away.

"GIVE ME TIME," HE SAID BEFORE STANDING UP TO GREET the incoming ambulance, pulling on a pair of gloves as he walked.

Was it really that easy? Time? How much time? Would he suddenly just give her some big sign that everything was fine again, and they would be back to normal? Was time something that would eventually bring them back to that kiss and see if they had a future after all? Did Max actually want to find out if he could have a future with Dani?

HOURS AND DAYS PASSED, AND THE CHAOS THAT RULED each day was simmering down. Max stared at the patient board as he erased another name. Not a bad day for the good guys. He checked his watch. Thirty more minutes and then he could go home, shower, and maybe relax for half a minute before dinner and their nightly routine.

"Hudson, phone call."

"Take a message," he said, rubbing the back of his neck.

"Sign offs for you," Bobby said, handing him a stack of charts. "Is Kelley coming in?"

"Jules and Roberts, I think."

"So, you have daddy duty tonight?"

"Go away," Max said, setting the charts down and grabbing a pen. His stack was even bigger. He needed to stop taking patients and putting off his own charts if he expected to leave on time.

"She's calling from Africa," Alex said from the desk.

Max looked over his shoulder at the same time his cell phone started buzzing on his hip. He unclipped it, saw his dad's name pop up and debated which phone call he wanted to take first, if any at all.

Three days ago, he received a curt email from his father informing him that he would be returning in three days—today. He would resume his fatherly duties and be home in time for Jules to leave for work, not leaving the kids with Rani or Rosie. Max didn't bother replying.

"Hey," Dani said, walking up. "Can I run a patient by you?" she asked.

"In a minute," he said as his cell went to voicemail. He grabbed the outstretched phone. "Hello." If he was in a bad mood before, the look on his face probably turned it worse.

"Who is it?" Dani whispered to Alex.

"Africa," he said with a shrug.

"Yeah, I can't really talk right now." His phone started buzzing again. "I'm at work. I can't talk to you right now. Just call my cell in a couple hours." He hung up, and before he could even attempt to call his dad back, the ambulance bay doors opened, and Jules walked in carrying Brinkley and holding Baer's hand.

"What is going on?" Max asked, taking Brinkley from her.

"Did your dad call?"

"Twice. I was on the other line. His flight was supposed to arrive hours ago."

Jules didn't wait before heading down the hall to the lounge and away from everyone watching.

"Yeah. Well, he didn't get on that flight. Rani is at a friend's house. I couldn't wait any longer, otherwise I would have been late for my shift."

"What do you mean he didn't get on that flight?"

"He called. Said he tried you ten times."

"I've had back-to-back traumas."

"He said he wasn't going to make it back today. Call him."

The kids climbed onto the couch and Max handed over his phone for them to play with. Jules opened her locker. "I'm sorry," he said.

They were finally getting into a new routine, their schedules as uncomplicated as possible, the kids stable. Now his dad throws a wrench in everything, leaving everyone scrambling. Good thing kids were pretty oblivious.

"We can't keep going like this," she told him. It was the first time he'd seen her this ragged. Her normal collected demeanor was showing signs of wear. Not once had they struggled with their schedules or had she been frustrated with Max's lack of schedule. He just did whatever he needed to do for her without question.

"I know. I'll fix it, I promise." He opened his locker and shed his white coat as the door swished open and Dani walked in. His charts were going to have to wait until tomorrow.

"Just call your dad."

"I will. Can you sign off on Bobby's charts when you get a chance?" She nodded. "Go save lives. Come on double trouble," he said, taking his phone from the kids and picking up Brinkley. "Baer, climb aboard."

The boy hopped onto Max's back as he kicked his locker shut.

"Wait, switch me cars. I parked out front because we were in a hurry." Jules handed him her keys, and he used his spare hand to fish his keys out of his pocket.

"Say 'bye,'" Max said, and a chorus rang out.

"Bye babies," she said with a smile before rushing out of the room.

"Alright, what's for dinner?" Max asked with a smile and a wink at Dani before walking out of the lounge with little voices yelling out their favorite foods.

He nearly had both kids loaded up in the car, content with singing along to the radio when he saw Maine heading out the door with Dani. They were about to go the opposite direction, and he knew he had to steal the moment now or risk weeks of scheduling issues with Jules until his father did show up.

"Maine," he yelled, shutting the left passenger door. One kid buckled.

"I'm late, Max."

"I just need two seconds. Dani, can you do me a solid and watch the kids?" he asked, not waiting for a reply before jogging to catch up with Maine.

"What is it?" she asked.

"I need to switch to nights."

"You just got back, you're still recovering, and you want to add nights onto all of that."

"This schedule is killing us. I have to do what is best for my family and that's taking nights until I can get some other arrangements made. Jules and I can't overlap schedules."

"And Jules works days?"

"You would have to talk to her, but I think that's better for both of us and the kids. She'll agree."

"Turning into a regular Mr. Mom, are we?"

"Maine, help me out here. When I went to Africa, I had a kid and an ex-wife and no issues. I'm trying to figure it out one day at a time."

"Fine. I'll make some changes. Come back tomorrow at seven p.m."

"Thank you," he said before jogging back to the car.

"Everything okay?" Dani asked.

"Yes. You are a saint. What do you think, monsters? Should we treat Dani to dinner for doing us a favor?" he asked.

"Not necessary," she said.

"Yeah!" the kids yelled.

"I think the majority wins. We were debating between prime rib and mac and cheese," he joked.

"I have to go take care of something," she said, hesitantly.

"Then come on over whenever you're done." This was him trying, throwing out a lifeline, and showing a different version of Max than what she witnessed over the past week.

"Okay, sure," she said.

"Yeah!" the kids yelled again, and she laughed.

"Okay. Let's hope Mom cleaned the house before she came to work," Max joked and he didn't miss Dani's smile falter. He closed the last door on the kids. "See you soon," he said softly.

She nodded and backed away.

He didn't even know why he said that. Dani wouldn't be seeing the house he shared with Jules. Jules was living at the cottage while he camped out at the main house.

11

THAT NIGHT

Max glanced into the den to make sure everyone was playing nice before going back to the food. Mac and cheese, cut up hot dogs, green beans, and chocolate pudding. Gourmet dinner for five-year-olds.

His phone rang, and he glanced at the clock. Maybe inviting Dani over wasn't the best idea. Usually, his spur-of-the-moment choices weren't. He was throwing out a lifeline, taking a chance to see what feelings rose to the surface. If he continued to hold Dani an arm's length away, there was no way to know if his old feelings were still there, or if all he harbored was hurt and abandonment.

"Hey, Dad," he said, picking up the phone, stirring the cheese into the pasta. "Sounds like you missed your flight."

"Change of plans." It sounded like he changed his dinner reservation, not a cross-country flight.

"What happened? We can't keep doing this. Jules and I had a schedule based on you coming home today."

"Like what? A cozy romantic dinner?"

"No, like not having to scramble for childcare because

you weren't here. Our work schedule is dependent on not having a nanny 24/7." Max wasn't in the mood for his sarcasm. He just wanted answers.

"Why don't you have a nanny? It would be so much easier."

"Because I actually like spending time with my kid. Which is more than I can say for you right now."

"Don't be harsh."

"Then get on the plane and prove it because you have two kids here who are starting to wonder if their dad is ever coming home."

"I talked to Rani yesterday. She's fine."

"She's sixteen. Of course she's going to say she's fine."

The doorbell rang, and he heard the scurry of tiny feet running to the door. "Who is it?" they both yelled, using some semblance of restraint over just opening the door.

He couldn't hear the answer but then the lock flipped, the door opened and closed, and there was silence. Max turned off the burner and walked into the den, heading for the door to find Dani being dragged toward the fort the kids created.

"Whoa there," Max said. "Let the lady take off her jacket first."

"Who's there?" his father asked, like he was grilling his son about a job interview or his college application choices. He was already judging.

"Hold on," Max said into the phone. "Dinner's almost ready. Brinkley, want to talk to Dad?" he asked.

"Yes," she yelled.

"Max, I can't talk to her right now."

"Too bad," he said before handing over his phone to Brinkley. "Come with me," he said to Dani, turning back toward the kitchen. "Wine, beer, water, juice?" he asked.

"Wine."

Grabbing a glass for her, he pushed the open bottle her way before starting to dish up two identical kids' plates with food.

"Mr. Mom in action," she commented.

"Easy kids. Thank you again for the mini-rescue earlier."

"It was nothing. Definitely not worthy of dinner and free booze. What was that conversation with Maine about anyway?"

"I just need to adjust my schedule."

"I imagine it's tough with the whole co-parenting thing, especially if one of you always wants to be home."

"Yeah, I guess. It's not really that." He grabbed the two plates and carried them back into the den to a separate child-sized table in the corner, not in front of the TV. "Food. TV off," he said. Without complaint, Baer turned off the TV.

"Dad wants to talk to you," Brinkley said, holding out the phone to him. The kids sat down without complaint and began eating.

Dani smiled.

"Yeah," Max said, getting back on the phone while dishing up the little bit of remaining food into one bowl. He handed Dani a spare fork.

"She sounds fine," his father said.

"She's five. She's fine right now. When are you coming home?"

"It might be a couple more weeks."

"Some might consider this child abandonment."

"They are with their brother and in very capable hands."

"I can see you doing that to me, but you can't do that to Jules. Her responsibility lies in Baer, not in your children."

"She's never complained before."

"She would never complain in general. That's not the

point. Just figure your shit out or don't. Choose to be a part of your kids' lives or just leave us alone."

"Max," his dad said. "It's not that easy."

"Tell me why? Make me understand." He wanted to give his dad the benefit of the doubt that he was struggling with his own issues just as Max had been with his. Maybe his father didn't want to burden his son with his own emotional trauma with losing his wife or show weakness when he wanted his son to only see his strength. Max could understand that. If only his father would communicate what was really going on.

"When you lose a spouse and someone you love, then you'll understand."

"You seem to have moved on just fine. What's her name? Jasmine?"

"Rebecca. We broke up. This one is different."

"This one? Moved on already? If you knock her up too, don't come running to me. I have to go." Max didn't wait for an answer before hanging up. Picking up his glass, he drained the contents before refilling it. Finally picking up a fork, he looked at her.

"Want to talk about it?" she asked casually.

"My dad kind of up and left me, and by default Jules, in charge of his children. He was supposed to be back today and just decided to postpone a few more weeks. Found a new girlfriend."

"When did he leave?"

"While I was in Africa."

"Wow."

"Yeah." He took a bite. "Dinner of champions. Didn't want it to go to waste. I already ordered plenty of options from Crave," he told her looking at his phone. "Which should be here soon."

"Great."

He finally set down his phone and looked at her. "I'm sorry about earlier."

"You're going to have to be more specific."

"Point taken. I made a comment about Jules by the car, and I saw the look on your face."

"She's a big part of your life."

"But she's also not my whole life, and I probably give the opposite impression to people. It's just all I've known for a long time. The kids just know us together. I don't know what happens when they finally realize we're separated." Why did he use the word separate and not divorced? It immediately implied they were unfinished.

"Does she live here?"

"No. She lives in the house we shared when we were married." Coward to leave out the fact that it was right next door.

"The divorce was new when I left town. We didn't get a real chance to go through the normal avenues, splitting things up, etc. And now I'm back, and I know I'm just trying to survive each day. Jules is a saint and more than I deserve right now."

"You're lucky to have her."

She was being nice, but he could tell there was more she wanted to ask if only he opened the door a little farther to let her in.

His phone rang again and with a quick glance, he silenced it.

"I'm going to check on the kids. Food should be here soon. Feel free to open a fresh bottle of wine."

He walked out of the room, and she heard him talking softly. Maybe this was the new Max trying to make it work, but the moment was too easy. The conversation was too easy.

He might be talking but it didn't feel like he was saying much. She was opening another bottle of wine when his phone started vibrating again, and the name Carrie popped up.

She glanced away, refusing to think too much about it. Max has a life and a history. She's not dating him, they are definitely not in an exclusive relationship, and he definitely still has some secrets he's hiding behind.

"Okay, once they are finished, they are going upstairs to change into pajamas. If we time it right, they will be fast asleep, and we can eat in peace."

He laid the empty plates in the sink.

"Your phone rang again."

"Ignore it."

"Are you sure? You don't have to because of me." As if on cue, his phone rang again and then the doorbell rang. "You answer the phone, I'll get the door."

"Hi," he said into the phone as she walked away. "I was in the middle of something." His eyes never left Dani as she disappeared. He was an idiot. What in the hell was he doing juggling all these women?

"I have a couple minutes, and then I have to go." He held the phone away from his ear. "Carrie, I promise, I will call you later, and you can talk all you want." She was right. He had been ignoring her, so it was hard to trust his word. He also had left without a word to her.

"I think you got enough food to feed us for days," Dani commented, walking back into the kitchen with three bags. He smiled tightly at her.

"Yes, I have company over. A friend." He looked down, the universal sign to hide shame or embarrassment. He spent a good amount of time trying to avoid eye contact with Dani. "Can you just tell me about it later? I promise. Yes, I promise." He listened for a solid couple of minutes, once taking a drink of his wine, and finally looking up at Dani who was watching him cautiously.

"I can go," she whispered. He shook his head.

"Okay. Yeah. Okay. Bye." He hung up and took a deep breath.

"Everything okay?"

"I don't know. Not really. Let me get the kids in bed. Grab plates and dish us up some food. I'll be right back." She watched him walk away before starting to open cabinets in search of plates.

Max was glad the kids didn't put up much of a fight that night. He wasn't in the mood for ten stories and half-hour back rubs to get them to sleep.

"Max," Brinkley whispered in the dark as he was about to close the door.

"Yeah, princess."

"Do I get a party for my birthday?"

"Of course," he said.

"Don't forget it's next week. Remember?"

Oh, shit. "Yeah. We can talk about it in the morning. Go to sleep."

He closed the door and quickly pulled out his phone. It only rang once.

"Everything okay?" Jules asked.

"Brinkley's birthday is next week."

"I know. I already started planning."

"You didn't remind me."

"We have barely been in the same room with each other all week," she pointed out. "And speaking of, I got a memo that I'm off nights."

"We can talk about it tomorrow," he said.

"Are the kids in bed?"

"Yeah. Dinner just arrived."

"Poor thing has to eat dinner alone," she teased. He was quiet, slowly coming to a stop in the foyer. "You're alone, right?"

"Dani is here." Now it was Jules' chance to be quiet. "We invited her over for dinner."

"Big step."

"I'm just being nice," he said.

Ever since Max went back to work, Dani had rarely come up in conversation as they tried to figure out a new rhythm to their life. When they were together, it was either all about kids or heated like a couple of teenagers. They both knew it wasn't healthy, and part of Max felt guilty that he sprung dinner with Dani on Jules like that.

But his relationship with Jules didn't feel all that defined either. Divorced on paper, but what else? He couldn't help but feel a pang of jealousy that if the situation were reversed, he wouldn't be happy about Jules having a guest over, regardless of whether they were an old friend, or co-worker, or a new romance.

"Okay, well, leave the porch light on if you want me to go to my own house," she said. That was the signal they had developed a long time ago when they were just starting to "date." If the porch light was on, it wasn't safe to approach. Since he'd been home, he'd kept the porch light on, regardless of whether he knew she was coming over or not.

"Please don't," he said walking back toward the kitchen.

"Is that *Please don't start* or *Please don't go home in the morning?*"

"Don't go home. Come here."

"You might change your mind," she whispered, silently telling him maybe things would progress with Dani, and she would stay for a nightcap.

"I won't."

"Goodnight, Hudson."

"Goodnight."

He turned his phone on silent and set it on the entry table near the kitchen. "What do we have to eat?" he asked, walking in and picking up his wine glass.

He would have dinner with Dani, he would try to take steps to repair their friendship, but the whole time, he was already looking forward to Jules showing up in the morning.

12

THE NEXT MORNING

He hoped he wasn't dreaming, or if he was, he hoped he would never wake up. A warm hand slid over his stomach before slowly sliding lower.

"You're naked," a voice whispered in his ear. He sighed as the hand wrapped around him. When was the last time this had happened? The last time he was the one being propositioned unexpectedly instead of making the move himself.

He lazily reached back and fumbled to pull her closer, his hand dragging one of her thighs over his, reaching between her legs. Now she sighed.

"You're naked," he whispered back, one finger sliding against her, a magnet to her body.

They hadn't been talking unless it involved kids or work. They had barely had any waking hours alone together. But somehow in what little time they had, they lost hours of precious sleep for these moments of connection.

Her hand tightened around him, and he sunk two fingers inside of her. She gasped, and he smiled. He loved that sound. He tilted his head back, and with closed eyes, his lips found hers. He kissed her slowly, like it was their first kiss or their very last, like they had all the time in the world. His fingers matched the steal of his tongue, the slow swipe, the small, almost imperceptible flick.

Her hand slowed, and he took that moment to turn fully and cover half her body with his, his fingers never slipping from inside her, his thumb pressing down while his fingers curled inside. Her hips arched closer to his hand, and he smiled against her lips.

"Good morning," he whispered. She twisted her hand in his hair and pulled him back to her lips, deepening their kiss.

His free hand curved around her thigh and draped it over his hip as he opened her up and slid inside her effortlessly. They just laid there motionless, enjoying the moment where everything seemed still, and the quiet surrounded them.

How many times had it started this way? How many more days would they get like this? When would they jointly decide it was time to stop?

Today wasn't that day.

Slowly he started moving, subtle and lazy rolling on his hips, his lips on her neck, his hands framing her face. Her teeth nipped at his ear, and he moaned into her neck, picking up his pace.

"Max," she whispered against his lips before he kissed her again. "More."

He could do more. Her thumb brushed across his lips, and he nipped at it before wrapping his lips around the whole thing and sucking. Her head fell back, and she started moving with him.

He felt her clench around him and picked up his pace, his hands gripping hers, the uncontrollable need to just touch her everywhere, to feel her, to taste her. This would be his mind on drugs.

He rolled them, her knees on either side of his hips, then sat up, wrapping her legs around his back, hands on her hips, tiny thrusts up into her body. Her back arched giving him perfect access to tanned breasts, still perfect even after a baby.

With one hand bracing her lower back, he tangled his fingers in the hair at the base of her neck, holding on for dear life. His lips made a path from ear to neck to sternum before latching onto a pink nipple.

If it were always this good, why were they divorced, why were they not staying together?

"Max," she whispered. He knew that call. He waited every time for that moment.

"Look at me," he said. She opened her eyes, and with both hands on his shoulders, she gave herself over to him, mind and body. He felt her start to shake, her toes curling, fingers digging into his hair. "Cum for me," he whispered against her lips before he swallowed what could have been an awakening scream with his own mouth.

The passionate kiss slowed into a languid tease, both holding on to each other for support. Finally, he pulled back with a kiss to the corner of her mouth, her cheek, the back of her ear, her neck.

Jules sighed.

"Good morning," he whispered.

"Good night," she countered.

He was still inside her. How was it he could never get enough of her? If they didn't disengage soon, he was bound to want to go for round two, and he was pretty sure there were two kids about to wake up at any moment and come running for the bedroom, regardless of their compromising position.

"How was work?" he asked, still holding on to her.

"Actually, pretty quiet. What time did you get to bed?"

"I don't remember. Probably like three a.m."

She glanced at the clock. Just after seven. "Big party?"

"Couldn't sleep," he said.

"How long did Dani stay?" she asked casually.

"Left an hour after I talked to you." She didn't respond as he slowly laid back on the pillows, and she almost complained that he was no longer inside her. With one thigh draped over his, she leaned against him.

"I'm glad you're figuring it out."

"I don't know what I'm doing, Jules. I'm just trying not to be an asshole."

"Good luck," she joked. He squeezed her thigh, and she laughed. "You're not an asshole."

"But."

"But if you're serious about seeing if you and Dani can have a future, we need to seriously think about stopping this." She made a small wave between them.

His response was lacing his fingers with hers and bringing her hand up to his lips, kissing a knuckle, a nibble, then just holding it to his chest.

"Max."

"Hmmm."

"What do you want?" The sincerity in her voice, the hesitation in asking, the vulnerability she was showing, it clenched at his heart. What did he want? Was he playing it safe with Jules? They had it good, but was he holding her back by holding on to her? Did she want something more with him, or with someone else? Was she afraid to hurt him?

"I think I want a shower," he said.

Slowly he untangled their bodies, and without looking back, he walked toward the bathroom. He didn't want to see the look on her face. To see if it was relief or sadness.

13

2013

"What do you want?" he asked. It was a simple question that held so much more.

"Whatever you're having," she said, before turning her back to survey the room. She had no idea what prompted her to say yes to Max's last-minute request that she be his guest to some charity gala his grandmother was on the board of.

"Pretty please with sugar on top," Max had begged. "I have to go, and if you go with me, I won't be forced to talk to three hundred people I don't know or be set up with one of the many debutants that are dragged by their parents in hopes of scoring a rich husband."

"Well, when you put it that way, how could I let you suffer alone? In fact, it might even be entertaining," She grinned.

"Thank you," he said, kissing her cheek without a second thought. "It's black tie. A little cleavage and some leg would go a long way to keep my reputation intact," he said with a wink, before rushing out of the lounge. A second later, he popped his head back in. "I'll pick you up at seven."

Now, here she was in high heels, black floor-length dress

with an empire waist that barely allowed her to breath, a plunging neckline, and with the right swish in her stride, an ample amount of leg.

She'd never seen Max so speechless when she opened the door for him.

Now, he was back at her side holding out a glass of red wine, bringing her out of her thoughts. "I really appreciate you coming with me."

"Free alcohol and an excuse to dress up. Sounds like a win-win to me," she said with a smile. "And a chance to see you grovel and play rich boy is a plus, too."

He silently fake laughed. "Ha ha. Where'd you find the dress?" he asked, making no attempt to hide his blatant appraisal of her accentuated features.

"Same place you found your tux. The closet," she said.

"I've never seen you wear it before."

"I've never seen you in a tux." She held his stare until she thought he flushed slightly, then slowly looked away. "What are we here for, anyway?" she asked.

"One of the many charities my Grami supports. WCA. MADD. WHO. YMCA. BPD."

"Point taken."

"I show up when I'm summoned. Most of the time I'm on a shift, so I have an excuse to miss an event. To be in the family is to show up. I do just enough not to be excommunicated and keep my father off my back."

"Incoming," she whispered when she noticed his father's eyes land on them. Max took a long drink before slowly sliding his hand around her waist and pulling her flush against his side.

She looked up at him in question. He just looked at her with a serious face. Any outsider would think more into the moment, more into their relationship, than what was actually true. For a split second, she felt a flush along her skin, a tingle in her fingertips, and the heat of his palm through her dress.

"Maxton, so glad you could join us tonight," his father said, shaking his hand.

"It's my first night off in a while."

"Have you seen your grandmother yet?"

Max nodded. "When we arrived. You remember Jules, right?" he asked. His fingers tightened on her hip, his thumb swiping slowly across the fabric.

"Hello," his father said with a nod.

"Where's Justine?" Max asked casually. His stepmother was usually attached to his father's hip at these events.

"She's in charge of the auction." Max didn't say anything. "She told me that you volunteered."

"She asked nicely."

"Volunteered for what?" Jules asked.

"The auction," Max said casually.

"Like the MC?"

"Like an auction item," he said before looking down at her with a smile. "Do me a favor. Be the highest bidder." He kissed her cheek quickly before letting her go without another word and disappearing into the crowd.

Max didn't know why he agreed to this charade. Maybe it was to prove to his father that he wasn't just a doctor, maybe it was because he agreed to something Justine asked of him when his father was constantly riding him to join the family business?

Maybe it was because deep down he never had the attention he craved as a child growing up in an adult world, and for a few minutes, he would be the center of attention?

Maybe he wanted to show off for Jules?

"Thank you again for doing this," Justine said with a smile

when he approached the side table where she was standing. He kissed her cheek like a good stepson would do.

"Of course," he said casually.

"Who's your friend?" she asked, nodding to Jules who was still awkwardly standing with his father, both of them watching their dates.

"Jules. We work together."

"Not a girlfriend?" she asked.

He smiled, noncommittal. Let people believe what they want.

"You play a good game, Max Hudson, but you don't fool me."

"What you see is what you get."

"I hope it's more than that, otherwise some lucky girl will end up very disappointed tonight."

"Don't be so sure about that," he smiled at her, then winked. He knew what he was doing the whole time. A waiter walked by with a tray of champagne, and he snagged a glass.

"Please don't be drunk up there."

"I will be on my best behavior. I already embarrass my family enough with medicine," he drawled.

"They are not embarrassed by you."

"Disappointed."

"Nor that."

"Do tell, oh, wise one."

"Just an innocent bystander here. It's safe to assume most parents hope their children grow up to be like them and follow in their footsteps. Your father only knows one business. He doesn't understand why being a doctor means so much to you."

"And my grandmother is worried I will never get married."

"She might be more worried that your part of the family fortune will go to waste."

"What part of the family fortune?" he asked, looking at her. She glanced away quickly, realizing that she probably just gave away one insider family secret that not everyone knew.

"You're up next," she told him, shuffling some papers, then turning to someone else who had arrived at the table. Max watched her carefully. That was definitely not the end of that conversation. As far as he knew, what he currently had was all he would be getting, and he never complained.

"This is a great event," Jules commented, trying to make awkward small talk with his father as they both watched their dates interact across the room.

"My mother tends to outdo herself every time."

"She's lucky to have your support. Max has mentioned these events to me in the past. It's nice he was able to attend one."

"If I know my son, he deliberately volunteers for night shifts in order to avoid these events at all costs."

"Not tonight," she said.

"Rare occurrence. As well as bringing a date. How long have you two been seeing each other?" he asked.

"We're just friends."

"Hmmm," he said stoically, looking over at his wife and son.

Jules turned to him, unsure what to say. Max was her friend, her best friend. His father's reaction maybe indicated otherwise.

"Max and I have worked together for years. I was happy to be his plus one and support a good cause."

"Max doesn't get a plus one," his father said, glancing down at her. For a quick moment, she could see her friend in *his father's worn face. The look in his eyes after pulling a double and exhausted from all the bullshit.*

"Is it because he's betrothed to the princess of Athens or the heiress to the Wall Street tycoon?" Jules was joking but his father didn't see it that way. Why was she nervous or even care what he thought? She was just an unwanted plus one.

A waiter came by, and Jules plucked a glass of champagne off the tray. She took a drink, anything to take her away from the awkward situation.

"You're probably better than that last one. The brunette. Meg something." He looked at her. "Do you know her?"

"I do," Jules said. This was turning into way more information than she bargained for.

"Maxton doesn't know what he wants. It's my job to make sure he doesn't make a fool of himself," his father said, watching as Max Hudson was announced on stage. "Like now." Then he walked off.

Jules watched as Max strutted across the stage in his tailored tux. Did she just get insulted by his dad, or was it approval? And what the hell was Max doing on stage?

He was THE auction item. Not something tangible that he held on display. His body, his face, his time. Jules was frozen. That's what he meant. Be the highest bidder.

She slowly started walking closer through the crowd, completely unaware of her own body or the people around her. Was she going to bid on a date with Max? She missed what it was even for. Where was the money going?

He caught her eye, smiled, then winked. She couldn't help but smile back. What a sly fox to thrust her into something without any explanation.

The auctioneer was slowing down, there was more time between bids. Max gave her a wide-eyed look.

"Going once, going twice."

Jules' hand shot up; her paddle raised. "We have a new high," the auctioneer announced. She missed the daggers from a woman a couple tables over. Jules couldn't stop staring at Max, and he didn't stop grinning at her.

The room waited in anticipation to see if someone else would outbid her, but the room remained fixed on her.

"Going once, going twice... SOLD for ten thousand dollars to the woman in black," he yelled. Polite applause erupted, and Jules' eyes grew wide as she stared at Max in shock. She did not have an extra ten thousand just lying around for a rainy day.

"That was perfect," Max said, coming down off the stage and taking her hand.

"Max, I don't have ten thousand dollars," she whispered.

"Don't worry," he said. "I'll take care of it." He talked so casually about money.

"What did I win, anyway?" she asked, turning to look at him.

"Me," he told her matter of factly. All eyes were on them. The handsome bachelor and the lucky girl who snagged him from under their noses. A stranger to them all.

And then he kissed her.

14

PRESENT DAY

Max Hudson had kissed her first. Not on the cheek. Not a peck goodbye. Not an accidental or embarrassing lip touching moment as they hugged. Full blown lip on lip, with a little bit of tongue, extremely intentional, and in front of a bunch of people.

That's the first memory Max remembered when he would get an overwhelming urge to kiss Jules—surprising her when she least expected it—while she painted her toenails, or while she was staring intently at the TV watching March Madness, or in the produce aisle deciding which avocados to buy. The mundane tasks with Jules turned him on more than that black dress.

He would remember that nothing felt as right in the moment as kissing Jules in front of a room of strangers just to prove that he belonged to her, and he would do anything to keep her.

The small gasp of surprise, her lips trying to smile even as she kissed him back, her hand over his heart snaking under his suit jacket while her other hand intertwined their fingers.

"What did I win?" she asked.

"Me, if you'll have me," he told her.

And he meant every word of it, even when he was crazy enough to propose and confessed that it was selfish to even ask considering there was a million-dollar price tag that came with it. Even when she bravely brought up separating and divorce.

Together or separate, there was a part of him that couldn't let go of belonging to Jules for the rest of his life—not just through a connection with their son—but a feeling that soulmates talk about. The stuff he never believed in before.

That's all he could think about in the shower after she asked him what he wanted, because he still struggled to voice his deepest desire, even to her, for fear it wouldn't happen, or she would once again be another person to leave him, really leave him this time. He didn't feel brave enough. Saying he wanted her was just too basic, and he didn't want to be basic with her.

When he came out of the shower, she was lying on top of the covers of his king-sized, four-poster bed. He remembered her commenting that it looked like it belonged to kings and queens, not a ragged hospital doctor with a man bun. It was the first time she spent the night, after three bottles of wine, a quickie in the living room where they acted like a couple of horny teenagers who had no patience to make it to a bed, shedding clothes through the foyer without embarrassment.

"Hi," he whispered when she opened her tired eyes to look at him.

She'd slipped on a tank top while he was in the shower and was snuggled deep under the duvet in the middle of the bed.

"Hi," she said back.

"Go back to sleep."

"I will when you're gone."

"Kids."

"Cat nap," she smiled and closed her eyes. When she opened them a minute later, he was still standing there looking at her. "What?"

He shook his head. Not to avoid her question but because she was a gorgeous woman, her hair splayed over the pillows, taking up the whole bed, one tanned thigh outside the covers with hot pink toenail polish and tattoo hearts on her foot.

He shook his head because if he spoke words right then, he would tell her everything he was feeling, and he didn't know if she was on the same page.

"I have girls' night tonight," she told him to try and break the spell.

"Lots of girls' nights going on these days," he commented. She used to go out with him all the time. Now she was embracing her single life at full force, leaving him home.

She sighed. "I don't have to go."

"I didn't say that." He didn't want to hold her back from living her life. He finally pushed away from the dresser, turning to open a drawer and pulling out socks and a gray t-shirt, before walking back into the bathroom.

When he came back out his hair was actually styled, and he had chosen black slacks and loafers over jeans and tennis shoes. The simple t-shirt dressed him down a bit, but not much.

She eyed him curiously. "You look nice."

"Thanks."

"Hot date?" she joked.

"Just with a bunch of drunks and idiots playing with sharp objects." He gave her a small smile as he clipped on his pager and collected all the usual accessories: keys, name badge, phone. At the last minute, he popped in a lone piece of gum that was on the dresser.

"Fresh breath, combed hair, slacks..." she trailed off when he started walking over to her. She rolled to face him as he laid a hand on her bare thigh and leaned over, kissing her slowly.

He knew what she wanted to ask but his answer probably wouldn't be what she expected.

"Dressed to impress," she whispered when he pulled back slightly.

He kissed her quickly before standing up straight and heading for the bedroom door.

"Max, do you think we should be dating other people?" she asked, a little hesitancy in her voice.

He leaned against the door frame and looked at her. Was she asking because maybe girls' night was actually a real date, or the possibility of something else, and she didn't know how to tell him? "Is that what you want?" he questioned.

"When was the last time you wore slacks to work and did your hair?" she avoided. Was she afraid of his answer because it might mean they were over, or because it's what she wanted but couldn't bring herself to say it aloud?

"I never thought about it." He did his hair, he dressed up, because he wanted to feel confident. He wanted to feel good in case she decided to leave him. Every day it felt like something was slipping, and he just wasn't sure if it was slipping away or back to what they used to have.

She sat up in the bed, brushing the hair out of her eyes. At that moment, he wanted to go back to her, to call in sick, to beg her to tell him exactly what she was thinking. He didn't realize she was waiting for the same thing from him - giving him the space to be sure of what he wanted.

"Have fun with the girls tonight," he finally conceded.

"Max," she whispered.

He looked down at his shoes and ran a hand through his hair, purposely messing it up to his normal disheveled style.

"I wanted to impress you," he said with a sad shrug, looking at her. Then he turned and walked out of the room.

15

A FEW DAYS LATER

"What did we do last night?" Dani asked, opening one eye to the sunlight, suddenly remembering that she passed out on Jules' couch at some unknown time far beyond midnight. Or was it this morning?

"Drank way too much," a voice said. Dani looked down from the couch to see Jules lying there with an arm over her eyes.

Girls' night out was quickly becoming a thing around the hospital. Dani's welcome drinks turned into a sequel that had Max acting strange, and she wasn't a hundred percent sure why. When Jacque called up in desperate need of a night out the day before Brinkley's birthday, Jules hesitated.

"When was the last time we went out?" Jacque asked over the phone, catching Jules on the tail end of her shift. She really just wanted to go home, take a bath, and rest before lots of tiny humans invaded their space for a day.

"It's Brinkley's birthday tomorrow. I don't want to be hungover and useless."

"For one, she's not your kid, so let Mad Max take care of his sister. And two, since when do you choose a child and your ex-husband over your best friends?"

"Let me check with Max," Jules said as he happened to walk up to the admit desk with Meg in tow, trying to finish up all their charts and discharges so he could end his half shift. He pretended he didn't hear her. He'd been awfully quiet for the past few days.

"Jules, I caught that douchebag I was seeing on a date with one of his co-workers. All I want is to go out and get drunk and flirt shamelessly with men I will never take home."

"Fine," Jules agreed. "I'll rally the girls up."

"No boys allowed," Jacque told her.

"Pick me up at seven," Jules told her before hanging up the phone.

Max glanced up at her, and she nervously tapped on the counter, playing with her phone. He didn't say anything.

"Meg, Jacque needs back up," Jules finally said.

"Count me in," she said with a smile. "I'll text Dani."

"Turning into the three musketeers," Max commented. He didn't look at Jules, but she knew that tone in his voice.

"You okay with this?" she asked.

He waited for a long awkward pause, writing quickly in a chart, before tossing the pen on the desk, closing the chart, and looking up at her. "Fine by me." Then he walked off in his two hundred-dollar loafers and custom fitted slacks. It was his new signature look and move—a quick one-liner that didn't really answer the question and just left her guessing.

Meg raised an eyebrow. "What Max is this?"

"Don't know, and I don't think I care," Jules said. "It's girls' night. Let's wrap this up."

They started at Juniper for happy hour and appetizers

before moving across to Diablo & Sons for tacos and tequila shots. It started getting fuzzy after that, except when they passed Strange Love, and Jules was stopped by an older high school friend who offered them VIP passes upstairs for free. There was dancing and more shots, and Jules had a vague recollection of sending Max naughty text messages but was too afraid to look and see.

"I feel like I just fell asleep," Dani said, bringing Jules back to the present.

"Four hours ago."

"You are a bad influence on me." She smiled but didn't open her eyes. "Did everyone else leave?" Dani asked.

"I think so. I don't want to move."

"Do you remember kissing that guy?" Dani asked her.

"Did not."

"Yeah. You did. A lot."

"Oh, God," she groaned. "I'm never drinking again." What possessed her to kiss someone else last night? Was it to see if it was time to really move on? Was she cheating on Max by kissing some guy at a bar? Was it some guy they worked with? "Wait, are you sure that wasn't you?"

"Maybe," she mumbled. No maybe about it.

In a far-away place, a phone started to ring. It felt very distant until Jules reached under the pillow at her head and produced her phone, putting it to her ear.

"Yeah." The laughter on the other end was not welcomed. "Shut up."

"I take it damage control is in order," Max said on the other end.

"What do you want?" she asked. He seemed awfully happy and upbeat after his pouting the past few days. His cold shoulder was starting to freeze their broken relationship in its cracked pieces. But his cheerful demeanor now either meant he was high on happy pills, drunk, or she most likely talked to him last night and had no recollection.

"We're cooking up breakfast. I'll make you my famous Bloody Mary. Change your clothes, brush your teeth, and get over here."

"Can't move."

"Yes, you can. It's Brinkley's birthday. She wants to know where you are."

"Shit." Maybe that's why he was happy. He started laughing again. "I'm not alone." The other end was silent. Jules risked a side glance at Dani watching her. It didn't even occur to her that Max would immediately assume it was a man.

"I'm going home," she whispered. Jules shook her head.

"Dani's here," Jules clarified.

Her heart started beating a little faster as she waited for him to respond. "The more the merrier. See you in fifteen." He hung up. Oh, Max.

"I'm not going to be the third wheel," Dani said, sitting up with a hand to her head.

"You are not the third wheel. We'll be even numbered. Plus, I could use a wingwoman. It's going to be a long day. Feel free to bail at any point, but at least have a Bloody Mary."

"I thought you weren't drinking."

Jules smiled. "You haven't had Max's Mary."

"That sounds sick and wrong."

Jules laughed before groaning at the pain in her head. Fifteen minutes later Jules slipped on a pair of sunglasses and flip flops and opened the front door. They'd downed pain pills and chugged water. If she didn't get there soon, Max would show up at the doorstep.

"Are you sure I should be joining you?"

"Max is a big boy." Jules made it sound like he was sharing toys, not trying to pick which woman he wanted to spend the rest of his life with. Of course, Dani didn't know she had been the topic of conversation many times with Jules and Max.

"In the past few weeks, he has not seemed that interested in being my friend, let alone something else. I get the same treatment as the garbage man. I just wish I knew what was going on."

"Don't we all. And you're not the garbage man. He's just a teenage boy working out his hormones." Jules on the other hand did not discuss Max much with Dani and how she was struggling with her own interpretation of his behavior.

"That analogy doesn't help. And why does it feel weird to be talking about dating your ex-husband with you? Not that I'm saying I want to date him, I'm just saying it's weird. Max kissed me once the last time I saw him. We really have no history." She stopped suddenly in the middle of the driveway and looked around. "Where are we?" Dani asked. They were surrounded by tall trees and only a paved drive that curved out of sight.

"My house."

"In the middle of nowhere?" she asked. "How did we get here?"

"I think maybe Max picked us up. Or Rani. Don't remember."

"Definitely not drinking like that again anytime soon," Dani commented. "Or ever."

"Let's go." Jules closed the door and stepped off the porch to the driveway. "And it's not weird, so don't worry about it. What's weird is suddenly kissing your best friend then marrying him and having his baby when not once in almost ten years did it even occur to me that Max Hudson would be a viable relationship partner for me."

"Good point. We're walking? That was not part of the deal." Dani was ready to pull out her phone and call an Uber so she could go back to lying horizontal.

"Well, I don't think either of us has a car here." Without further explanation Jules slipped through a break in the trees and disappeared. Without any other option Dani quickly followed after her, immediately coming to a halt.

"Jules, that's Max's house."

"Yep," she said without an explanation, continuing to walk around to the backyard. Maybe she should have been a little more forthcoming about her situation with Max. There were days even Jules wondered if she was the garbage man, keeping all the trashy secrets to herself and hiding them from everyone, especially Dani.

She saw unknown faces setting up four different types of bounce houses and a caterer covering tables. Balloons were strung on every surface. The flowers were freshly watered, and a carpeted walkway to the back was being staked down with pink princess staffs.

"Jules, why didn't you tell me you lived next to Max?"

"It never came up," she said with a shrug and a smile that begged for forgiveness.

"Easy conversation starter. So, I live next to my ex-husband. That's not weird at all." She was being sarcastic. They can just chalk up this whole past twenty four hours as weird.

"I got the house in the divorce. It's paid for. Who am I to argue?"

"You're like the modern-day Bruce and Demi."

"With more hair. Just act natural." Dani laughed as Jules opened a back door into the house.

"In the prep kitchen," someone told Jules before walking off.

"Do they service your house, too?" Dani asked, noticing they were surrounded by all types of help running around.

"Hell, no. Just the landscaper." Dani was not prepared for what was behind door number one when Jules pushed it open.

"Perfect timing," Max said as he garnished two-pint glasses with an asparagus stock and a piece of candied bacon. He held out both drinks to the women with a smile.

"You could have at least put some clothes on," Jules said with a smirk, taking her drink.

There was Max standing in the middle of the kitchen barefoot in dark grey joggers and nothing else. Squeals of Mom and Jules rang out through the kitchen, and they both winced.

"Pull up a stool," Max said to Dani more than Jules and lifted his own glass to his lips. "The fun is just beginning."

***

MAX SAT BACK IN HIS CHAIR ON THE LAWN AND WATCHED Jules walk away.

The birthday party was a success as the kids were in the middle of a heavy sugar crash that he hoped lasted twelve hours so he could enjoy some extra hours in peace. Jules offered to cover the night shift at the hospital, leaving Max with caterer and party clean up, plus the children.

She hadn't intended it to be the perfect opportunity to force Max alone with Dani, who happened to already have the night off. She just wasn't sure she was ready to be alone again with Max for the night.

"I should go, too," Dani said, moving to stand when Jules tossed her water bottle in the trash.

"No, you don't," Jules told her. "Keep Max company. Help him procrastinate in cleaning up after twenty kindergartners."

Max just looked at Jules behind his sunglasses but didn't agree or disagree. If she wanted to push the matter, then he was just going to let her do it. If she needed to make sure he gave ample time with Dani to determine if she was worth pursuing, then he would let her believe that. He was already starting to believe deep down that no other woman would be his Jules.

"Is this a ploy?" Dani asked once they were alone, handing him a beer from the cooler on the deck.

"Probably." He took a long drink and glanced over at her. "Afraid to be alone with me?"

"No. Are you?"

He looked away. "Nope."

"You gotta help me out here a little bit," she continued after the pause went on too long.

"With what?"

"Are you mad at me? Hate me? Wish I would just disappear again?"

"No," he told her. When she didn't respond, he looked at her. "At one point, honestly, yes, I was mad, maybe I thought I hated you. But that was years ago. Not now."

"What is it now?"

"I don't know," he said looking back at her.

"Is it Jules?"

"No."

She laughed a little. "The short answers are not helping at all."

"I'm sorry." He sighed and ran a hand through his hair.

"I'm just not used to this anymore. Small talk, casual conversation. I'm familiar with silence, the life I used to have, and not the life I came back to."

"What do you mean?"

"I don't have my shit together. It may look like it most of the time, but really, I'm just trying to survive each day. Sometimes I'm taking it hour by hour, which is progress, because when I got home, I was in the minute-to-minute arena. Sometimes all I have are short answers."

"Because of Africa."

"Africa, and my family, and almost dying, being back in a society. I forgot what it was like to have internet and telephone service at my fingertips. To be in immediate contact with the people I loved, to have any choice at my beck and call—food, conversation, supplies. I ran away to nothing, and when I came back it was all so... different."

"You were gone for a year?"

"Almost. Here and there. I came back once because of visa issues, to get supplies, see Baer. Jules brought him to Europe once."

He took a long drink of his beer.

"Max," she said. He looked over at her, his crystal blue eyes darker in the fading sun and haunted from his inner shadows. "When I decided to come back, it was partly because the job was too good to pass up, and I was ready for a change. A bigger part of the decision was because I left without ever knowing what would happen between us." She let that sit. "I'm not going to run away from that now, but if there is someone else, then just tell me. If it's Jules or Meg or some intern on the third floor, it doesn't mean we can't be friends, that we can't get back what we used to have as friends. Because you were my best friend, and I miss my best friend."

He kept her gaze for as long as possible before finishing his beer and resting his elbows on his knees and dragging his hands through his hair.

"I'm not the same person I was before. I have a lot of baggage, and I have a lot of demons. I don't ever want to be someone that causes you pain."

"Welcome to the club."

"You don't want to be in this club." He gave her a sideways glance. Not a moment later, Rani cleared her throat as she poked her head out the back door.

"Decent?" She grinned at him.

"If you don't come bearing provisions, you're not allowed," he said.

She smiled and held up a six pack.

"Can I go to Jessica's?" she asked.

"Where are Thing 1 and Thing 2?" he asked.

"In your bed, bathed and brushed, watching *Finding Nemo*, basically already passed out."

"Bring the beer, and you can go."

She smiled and bounded down the porch like only a sixteen-year-old could, handed him the beer, kissed his cheek, then disappeared.

"Best brother award goes to you," Dani said, finishing her own beer. He opened two more and handed her one. "Thing 1 and Thing 2? Your kids have names."

"Brinkley is my sister," he clarified. "Besides, it's more fun this way. They were born a few months apart. Sometimes it's hard not to look at them and immediately think of twins."

"I did the first time I saw them."

"As does the rest of the world. It's easier that way. The Things. Mini Monsters. Evil Twins. Double Trouble. The list is endless."

"Where's her mom?"

"Died. Rapid breast cancer when Brinkley was three."

"Enter the best big brother in the whole wide world."

"I think that award is a more recent accolade."

"Care to share?"

"Ever heard of conscious uncoupling?" That was not the way she thought the conversation would go.

16

———

2017

"Ever heard of conscious uncoupling?" Jules asked.

Max stopped mid-stride and looked at her. "What are you talking about?"

"It's the new, hip thing to do." He just looked at her behind his sunglasses. They had finally had a chance to take a five-minute break at work to get outside and grab coffee. This was how she wanted to spend it.

"I'm not hip."

"I know a teenager who would beg to differ."

Max didn't say anything and started walking again. She grabbed his arm.

"Will you stop walking and just talk to me?"

"What do you want me to say?"

"Are you pouting?" She smiled at him, and when he didn't smile back, she laced her fingers in his and dragged him to the nearest bench.

"What's changed?" he asked.

"Nothing. Nothing has changed."

"Then why now when everything is so good."

"*Well, for one, we always said this wasn't forever.*"

"*Maybe I want you to be my forever,*" he said. He was being honest, but it wasn't something they ever talked about, so he could understand why she might not believe it.

"*No, you don't.*" He didn't argue with her. They never argued. They never disagreed. They were always on the same page. He always let them be on the same page.

"*What's your second reason?*"

"*I love you but being married kind of cramps our style.*"

Was she really doing this? Were they really talking about breaking up when inside and out they had the perfect marriage? He knew it was a deal in the beginning, but he stopped thinking of their marriage as a "deal" after Baer came into their lives.

"*Who?*"

"*There is no one else but being married stops any other person from showing up.*"

"*Okay,*" he said softly.

"*Not okay. You don't get to okay me. This is your life, too. I thought we had an agreement, I thought we were always on the same page.*"

"*We were. We are.*" He clarified, glancing at her.

"*Then what is really bugging you?*"

"*It just feels like I've failed. I can't even succeed at a marriage that was agreed to on a whim so I could inherit my trust fund. Boy will my dad get a kick out of this one. My fake marriage.*" When he proposed to Jules, he finally confessed the more deep-seated disappointment his father had in his decision to follow medicine. He had tried everything to convince Max to change his mind. In the end, it was an ultimatum—marry, produce an heir, or switch careers to the family business— otherwise his trust fund would go down the drain.

"*For the record, you did succeed at your original fake*

marriage, and furthermore, there was nothing fake or arranged or unwanted about the past four years."

"Grami is probably rolling over in her grave right about now."

"Do you regret anything?"

"No," he told her.

"Then how have you failed, and how has it been fake?"

"I benefited with large sums of cash to marry you, and subsequently have a child with you, which I was rewarded for. And now it's going to be over. Did I falsely advertise? Did I forget to tell you something about the benefits of the arrangement?"

"No. I like to think I benefited from it as well," she pointed out. "How would you have felt if you never got married and never had a son before Grami died? Like you missed out on the family fortune? Poor? Homeless? Depressed? Would you have really quit being a doctor to crunch numbers?"

"No."

"I could have said no to you and flat-out refused your proposal. You didn't hide it from me, you laid out all the facts, and I was in a position to accept. I regret nothing about the past three years being married to you. No regrets in general."

"And now you're not in a position to keep up the facade."

"There is no facade. When people think of a marriage, what do they see?"

Max just looked at her like she was playing a stupid game or trying to teach their kid rational thought. He was a doctor, not a toddler.

"Two people who love each other. Live together. Have some kids together. Spend all their time together. Argue together. Sleep together."

"You made your point."

"I don't think I have because you still look like a kid who lost his puppy."

"I'm allowed to be sad about it."

"Okay. How about this? What really changes?"

"Divorced people don't live together, don't sleep together, don't do things together. And they certainly don't have crazy sex in the laundry room together."

"Would that glum face go away if I told you there's no rule book that says we have to be those divorced people?"

"What are you talking about?"

"Someday, some boring man is going to come along and knock my socks off. And some bombshell is going to walk around the corner of this hospital, and you will turn into a blubbering idiot. But until that time, I see no reason not to carry on like we used to, as the mood strikes."

"The mood strikes me a lot," he said with a smirk as he pulled their entwined hands to his lips and kissed the back of her hand before standing up and pulling her with him.

"Maybe temper the mood down a bit. We're definitely not newlyweds anymore, and we probably should keep it between the two of us. We don't need the whole hospital knowing the details of our living arrangements, separation, or the sex."

"Where am I going to sleep when you decide to bring said man home with you?"

"Maybe we start splitting time between the cottage and the mansion. We already have a lot of split shifts so that Baer isn't stuck with a nanny 24/7."

"If we tell all our friends and my father that we are divorced, they will think we are crazy, because people who don't hate each other never get divorced."

"Conscious uncoupling. We are not in love with each other. To some people that's all the reason they need. Besides, who gives a damn what other people think."

"*How do you know we're not in love?*"

"*Max,*" she whispered.

"*You can have the cottage.*"

"*I thought I was always going to get the cottage.*"

"*People are going to think this is weird.*"

"*We'll deal with it when we get to it. For now, no one has to know.*"

"*Everyone will know. You can't keep a secret from this place.*"

17

2014

"Everyone will know. You can't keep a secret from this place." Those were his famous last words before they got in their separate cars in the driveway of their house to go to the same workplace, days after being secretly married on vacation.

"It's been ten days. No one will know."

"They will if you don't take that ring off," he said. "See you at work. I'll pick up coffee."

"Wouldn't want to be showing up at the same time."

"Bye," he said with an eye roll before closing the door to his Range Rover and pulling out ahead of her. He felt awkward suddenly. It's not like this was the first time they left for work at the same time from this house. Being married suddenly took on a whole new vibe, and he had no idea how to act normal.

He probably jinxed them. He never should have said those words or taunted fate. He should have predicted his Grami and her ploys over his own. She would never ask his permission to take an ad out in the paper for any reason, why would the announcement of his nuptials be any different. High

society still demanded such classy things as printed announce-
ments in the paper for the world to see.

Six days ago, they got married. Two days ago, they told his
family. He wouldn't be so lucky to go back to work and everything would be normal.

"Morning," he said, walking through the ambulance doors
to the front desk, flashing his keyed badge to get through secu-
rity, coffee carrier in hand and sunglasses still on.

"Someone got some sun," bouncer, desk clerk, jack of all
trades Alex announced.

"A ten-day vacation will do that for you," he said, writing
his initials on the board indicating he was on deck to take
patients. Without hesitation, he wrote Jules' initials down, too.
It was not out of the ordinary. He did it almost every single
day they started a shift together.

Like getting coffee, eating lunch in the lounge, finishing
each other's sentences, and occasionally carpooling.

"Get caught up on the news while you were away?" Alex
asked casually with a suspicious smile, holding up the paper.

"I got my own," he said, pulling the paper from under his
arm. "What'd I miss?"

"Just the same old drama, day in and day out."

"Great. Who's on?" he asked, glancing at initials but not
sure if they were coming or going.

"Maine takes over for Meg at five. You and Jules are
running point. Kelley is off in five. Bobby, Jared, and Jenners
are with you. And the new interns."

"Of course she would schedule new interns for my first
day back."

"Joys of management."

"Okay. Tell Kelley to find me for rounds."

"You got it."

Max rounded the desk and headed down the hall, pushing

open the lounge door with his free hand. Jules was already in there with Bobby and Jenners.

"There are patients on the board. What are you doing sitting in here?" Max asked, offering the tray of coffee to Jules. She took her cup and then set the tray on the table.

"Just catching up on all the news and vacation adventures," Bobby said with a wink.

"Nice tan," Jenners said.

"It's called ten days on a beach. You didn't think we'd waste a real vacation sitting inside, did you?" Max said, opening his locker.

"We?"

Max looked at Jules then at their colleagues. "Yeah."

"I thought you went to the beach with friends," Bobby said to Jules. Not that the hospital gossip mill wasn't in full swing placing bets that Max and Jules were together after his sudden request for time off.

"What am I? Chopped liver?" Max asked as he pulled a scrub top from his locker and slid it over his white t-shirt.

"I was with friends," Jules explained half-heartedly.

"There are so many other eligible bachelors that you could have taken to the beach. If anything, just the sight of Max would have intimidated any man from even approaching you. How dare you do a disservice to your friend like that," Jenners said, pointing at Max.

Max grabbed his coffee with a laugh. "I'll have you know, I am a great wingman. Let me know next time you're going out, I would be happy to help you capture your own Prince Charming," he told her.

"I'd probably catch something, that's for sure," Jenners said sarcastically.

"Hey," he said. It might have been a long-running joke, but it was an incorrect one that still haunted Max years later. It pre-dated Jules, Meg, and Dani, and yet it still followed him around. The joke that he was the rich bachelor who slept around, searching for the perfect wife for his perfect life.

One: His life wasn't perfect. Two: He never slept around. He was monogamous to a fault and pickier than most women.

"I've got nothing to prove. I was just offering as a friend," Max said, looping his stethoscope around his neck.

"Like a friend with benefits?" Bobby said.

"Geez, what is this, Rag on Max Day? At least let me drink my coffee before I have to start fighting back," he said, tossing the paper onto the table.

"Are you done with that?" Jenners asked, looking at the paper.

"No, I have," he looked at his watch, "three minutes before my shift starts. Need to catch up on all those stocks and bonds." He pulled out a chair and sat down scanning the headlines.

"I'll take care of rounds," Jules said.

"Fresh interns. You can take those as well," Max said with his most charming smile.

"In your dreams." Jules walked out one door as the opposite door opened, and Meg walked in.

One look and Jenners and Bobby grabbed their coffee. "I got a patient," they both said before disappearing. Max glanced up and saw her standing in the room. Just the two of them and she didn't look happy.

"You son of a bitch," she said.

"What?" he asked as if nothing had happened.

She threw the paper in her hands at him nearly spilling his coffee. He opened the single page to see the wedding announcement, including a photo of him with Jules. He remembered that photo. It was right after Jules won him at the auction for ten thousand dollars. Sly old lady. He smiled and shook his head. She one upped him this time for sure.

"You think this is funny?" she yelled.

"Meg," he said, putting the paper down and standing up.

"I wasn't good enough for the family money."

"This has nothing to do with money." Not completely.

"And I believed you the other 800 times you told me Jules was just your friend."

He was about to say that exact same thing and realized it wasn't true. She was his wife. Arrangement or not, he needed to keep reminding himself. Even if they weren't married, he was still sleeping with her, they were still in a relationship, and that was enough. They had spent so much time saying 'just friends' that to acknowledge that Jules was anything else was foreign.

"Meg," he started again but already knew it wouldn't go anywhere.

"You made a fool out of me, Hudson."

"This isn't about you."

"Everyone with half a brain knows the rules of the riches. Marry someone respectable to the family to inherit the fortune."

"As I said, this isn't about money."

"What is it about then? Because if my memory is intact, six months ago I was the one in your bed."

The door opened, and Kelley walked in. "Hate to interrupt this lovers quarrel, but I need to take off," she said, walking to her locker.

"It's fine," Max said softly, picking up his coffee and the wedding announcement. "Come with me," Max said, opening the door and politely ushering Meg through it and down the hall to the back exit.

"Why would you do this?" she asked the second the door closed, and they were alone.

"Meg, shit happens. Life happens. Good and bad. You know the place I was at when you showed up in my life. I was pissed and hurt, and all I wanted was someone to make me feel better. I told you that. It was shitty, but it was true."

He never wanted to hurt her, and he was definitely extremely selfish. He did not take her into account when his relationship with Jules changed. He didn't think of Meg when he proposed. He didn't think of Meg at all. He thought she was fine, a little pissed, but being in a shitty rebound relationship was worse than being alone.

She didn't respond, just watched him. Waiting for something.

"Jules just happened. I didn't seek it out, I didn't expect it at all. The money is the money, but whether I have it or not, does not matter to me. I know that might be hard to believe. There was just a moment where things looked clear to me, and I was just sitting there, and I was happy, and I don't really remember the last time I was just... happy."

"Did you even try with me?"

"I was a selfish asshole with you. I never meant to hurt you, and that was all I did. You were great and amazing and the only person at that time who made me forget for half a second that I wasn't a complete loser. I was throwing a pity party, and it's like you were the clown."

"Thanks," she said sarcastically.

"I'm sorry. I didn't think this would hurt you. I didn't think you would really care. You were just as unhappy as me, and there is definitely someone else out there who will give you the moon and the stars. But it's not me, and I'm sorry."

"So now suddenly you're married to Jules, and no one even knew you were dating."

"I don't expect people to understand, and if you really need me to go through it with you, I will. Despite everything, how I treated you, the way I was when we met, you saw me at my lowest. You stood by me while I figured myself out. You gracefully let me go. And you got to witness first-hand the drama my family could cause. They were not nice to you. You know more than everyone else. People will make their assumptions, and I know you have as well."

"I know it's not about me. I'm sorry, too, but it's hard to be the girl left behind. No matter how people see it, and no matter what you tell them, in the span of half a year, we broke up and now you are married. Both very public and personal matters in our workplace."

"I give you permission to tell anyone who asks whatever you want. I will be the bad guy any day. I just don't want you to be hurt over this. I know I can't expect you to be okay right away. I want us to be okay as friends, as colleagues. I don't want you to be upset with Jules. It's a big ask, and I will do anything to help. Consider me on my hands and knees begging."

The side door opened, and Jules poked her head out.

"We have an incoming." They looked at her.

"Okay," Meg said with a nod to Max. "Okay."

Then she walked toward Jules and through the door.

"Okay?" Jules asked him as he took one last sip of coffee and tossed it.

"Grami posted our nuptials in the paper," he said, handing her a copy. "Damage control."

18

PRESENT DAY

"You should meet her. We should all go out," Marco said a couple days later at work.

"Who is we?" Max asked, leaning against the wall. The sun was out, he wanted to be anywhere but work. He'd resorted to scrubs and a t-shirt to keep cool as the summer heat was messing with their outdated AC, and he hated dry cleaning the amount of slacks he was going through.

"Whoever you want. Jules, Dani, whoever."

"And who would you be bringing?" Max asked. "The candy striper? Can she drink?"

"Very funny. She's old news."

"I can't keep track anymore."

"You're one to speak. One minute it's Jules, then I hear you have Dani over a couple nights ago."

Max ran his hands through his hair, in desperate need of a haircut. "Maybe I'll be celibate for a while," he said with a shrug like it was actually an option.

"Now that's a joke. When was the last time you were *celibate*?"

"When I was sixteen?" Max grinned.

"Exactly."

"I mean sometimes it was just me, myself, and I, but it was still a wonderful experience."

"Why don't you and Jules just get back together and actually be together?"

"You say that like we weren't 'actually together' when we were married," Max said with air quotation marks.

"We know there was more to it than just that." Max had confided in Marco on occasion about the pressure of marrying, of having a child, all to make his family happy and inherit some fortune he wasn't sure he wanted. "Honestly, Jules deserves better," Max said.

"Better than you? Have you seen you?"

"Stop hitting on me," Max said. "Stick to candy stripers."

"Man, you need to get your mojo back. I think you left it in Africa. You have girls swooning over you for days. Jules is lucky to have you. You might be an idiot sometimes, but you're a catch. But so is she. I'm surprised she hasn't moved on either. That says something."

"Let me get this straight. You think I should be trying to make it work with Jules. Not Dani."

"Are you really trying with Dani?"

"I'm not trying with anyone."

"You've been spending time with Dani outside of the hospital."

"As a friend. Trying to forgive her for breaking my heart."

Marco rolled his eyes at Max's near teenage dramatics. "You basically live with Jules. You come to work together. You go home together. You stare longingly at each other over patients."

Now it was Max's turn to roll his eyes. "I'm just living my life."

"Exactly. Just go with the flow and see what happens."

"There has to be some rule that says while you are trying to figure out what woman to spend the rest of your life with, you probably shouldn't be having sex with anyone."

Marco shrugged. "Matter of opinion."

"So, who are we double dating with?" Max asked.

"Just a girl."

"It's never just a girl if you want us to all go out together."

Marco smiled at him before tossing his cup in the trash and heading for the doors.

"Right," Max said, watching his friend walk away.

What did he want? It used to be so simple. Now it was just complicated. He had a huge crush on Dani, he pined after her like a little puppy dog for a whole year, he was devastated when she left. But Dani leaving opened the door to him finding Jules. Was Jules the easy way out or the forever dream? Was Jules just comfortable and routine, or was she the missing piece?

"Penny for your thoughts," Dani said, breaking into the silence.

"Hey," he said.

"On a break?" she asked.

"Yeah," he glanced at his watch. "Apparently a long break."

"We have an OD coming in. Three minutes. You're safe."

"Thanks."

Why was this awkward? They had a great night after Brinkley's birthday. It almost felt like they were on the road back to normal. But at work, it felt forced. He had so much history in this place. He had his anger with her leaving, he had Meg, he had Jules, he had Africa.

"Can we talk later?" she asked.

"Yeah," he said. She handed him a set of gloves as they heard the approaching sirens. Time to get to work.

"HUDSON, YOUR SISTER CALLED," ALEX SAID WHEN THEY walked out of trauma, tossing away gloves and gowns.

He instinctively reached for his cell to find his pocket empty and remembered it had died sometime in the early morning of his double shift.

"What'd she want?"

"Something about one of the kids falling and bringing them in."

"What do you mean someone falling?" Max asked rhetorically not waiting for an answer before walking into the lounge and pulling his phone off the changer. Four missed calls from Rani. Three from his dad.

He was mid-dial back and halfway to the desk when the doors opened, and the outside world faded as he saw the pink tulle dress on the gurney. Rani was right behind carrying Baer.

"What happened?" Max asked her.

"Six-year-old fall on the playground. Loss of consciousness," the paramedic said.

"I'm so sorry, Max," Rani said. Max took Baer from her, his cheeks still tear streaked in fear for his best friend.

"Where's Jules?" Max yelled, but no one answered. Dani stood and watched as he tried to manage this defining moment in his life.

"I'm sorry, Max," Rani whispered.

"Take her to Trauma 1," Max yelled. "It's okay," he whispered, pulling Rani to him with a kiss to the temple. "Take Baer," he said, handing over his son.

"Daddy," he cried.

"It's okay," Max said, brushing a hand over his head before running down the hall toward Brinkley.

She seemed smaller on the gurney than he would have imagined.

"She's waking up," someone said.

A little disoriented, Brinkley whispered, "Daddy" before her eyes focused on her big brother at her side. "Max?"

"It's okay. I'm right here," he whispered, brushing a hand over the top of her blonde locks. "Talk to me," Max called out to anyone who would listen.

A barrage of orders followed as Max stayed eye to eye with the little girl. "Where is Jules?" he finally asked.

"She's upstairs with a patient. We paged her," Maine said, suddenly appearing and taking over as point for the residents and interns. "Where does it hurt?" she asked.

"My head and my arm," Brinkley said.

"How about your belly?" Maine asked softly, pressing along all the point places.

"No."

"Good. Let's do an x-ray of her arm and rule out a head injury," Maine said. "Do you know what happened?" she whispered to Max.

"No. Rani was with her."

"We need to find out."

"I'm not leaving her," Max hissed.

"It hurts, Max."

"I know, baby," he said. "I'm right here."

"What happened?" Jules asked, pushing through the doors.

"She fell on the playground. Can you go talk to Rani and find out the details?" Maine asked, stopping her within a few steps.

"Max." Jules said, and he turned to look at her, all the pain Brinkley had was showing in his eyes. "It's okay," she told him.

"Go talk to Rani," Maine said.

Jules threw up her hands and nearly ran to the admit desk. Rani and Baer were sitting in the waiting area.

"Mommy," he cried, flying toward her.

"It's okay, baby. What happened?" she said, asking Rani more than Baer.

"B fell. I promise I didn't push her."

"I know, baby." Jules held him close. "What happened?" she asked Rani.

"They were playing tag like always. Running up and down the stairs and those stupid pathways. I didn't even look away. I didn't go anywhere. I was there the whole time, Jules. I promise."

"I know. I know." Jules stood up and pulled her into her arms, holding both kids.

"Is she going to be okay?" Rani asked.

"Max is with her. It's okay." Jules held her hand, and together they all walked back down the hall to the trauma room. Standing outside the doors, Jules watched them work and watched Max crouch next to Brinkley. At one point it looked like she smiled.

Jules tapped on the glass when things started to quiet down, and Max waved them in as he lifted the bed to tilt her up.

"Max, I'm so sorry," Rani said.

"It's not your fault," Max said, pulling her into his arms and feeling her start to shake with tears. "It's okay."

"She has a broken arm and I believe only a mild concussion," Maine said. "Great news that it's not worse. Let's monitor her for a couple hours, get her in a cast, and you guys can go home."

"Thank you," Max said.

"Max, take a couple days off. Jules, take the rest of the day," Maine said before walking off.

"What am I? Chopped liver?" Jules asked.

"Evil stepmonster?" Max joked.

"Very funny."

"Are you guys really doing this now?" Rani asked, wiping her eyes and pulling away from Max.

"What?" he asked.

"Flirting," she said disgustedly.

"That's not flirting," Max said.

"With you two? Yeah. It is." Max looked from his sister to his ex-wife. Jules shrugged. He winked at her. Maybe it was flirting for them.

"Okay, here's the plan, gang," Max said with a deep breath. "Brinkley is going to get a bright pink princess cast on her arm. We'll order pizza for dinner. And we're going to have one big slumber party and watch movies until we can't keep our eyes open."

"Cheese pizza," Brinkley and Baer yelled at the same time, like they hadn't just suffered some trauma.

"You got it. Rani, can you take Baer home?"

"No," he cried, gripping Jules tighter. She looked at Max.

"Okay," Max said softly, kissing his son's head. "Give us a second," he said, slowly walking out of the room with Rani. "This was not your fault," he told her. "You don't have to apologize. You don't have to feel bad. I see this day in and day out. Kids get hurt. Kids fall." He sensed the tears were about to fall again.

"Can you do me a favor?" he asked.

"Yes."

"Go home. Take a bath. Drink some tea. Relax. It's all okay. In two hours, order pizza and set up the fort."

"What home?" she asked. Max glanced into the trauma room where Baer and Brinkley were sitting on the same bed chatting away with Jules watching.

"What house do you want to go to?" he asked.

"Jules'."

"Jules' it is." He pulled her into a hug, kissed her cheek. "I love you."

"Love you, too, Max." She let him go then headed down the hall. He was about to walk back into the room when his phone rang. His father.

"Hi, Dad," he said casually, leaning against the outside door frame watching his family.

"Where have you been? I've been calling and calling."

"We had a little bit of an emergency, but everything's fine."

"Rani left me a frantic message crying because her sister was hurt."

"She's fine. A bump on the head and broken arm."

"Why weren't you there? You are supposed to be the responsible one."

Max took a deep breath. "You're right. I am the responsible one. I'm the one who is here. I'm the one who is doing everything for our family while you are off with your new toy."

"That is uncalled for. My job requires that I travel right now."

"What if I weren't here, Dad? What would you be doing with your children while you are off *working?*"

It was silent on the other end. Max saw Jules turn to look at him, and he couldn't help but smile. "Everything okay?" she mouthed.

He nodded. "When are you coming home?" Max asked. "It's the last time I'm going to ask."

He held his breath waiting for an answer from his father. "I don't know, Max."

"Goodbye, Dad," Max said and hung up the phone.

19

———————

A WEEK LATER

Max waited a week, waited until things went back to normal, for Brinkley to start sleeping through the night again, and then he made some decisions. If his dad wasn't willing to come home, even after an emergency room visit, Max needed to get to work. He never let himself think of how it might feel if he were no longer a parent or guardian to his sisters.

"What are you doing out here all by your lonesome?" Jules asked, finding Max on a bench with his cup of coffee and all his thoughts.

"Just taking a break." He patted the space next to him, and she sat down.

"Looked deep in thought."

"Nothing gets past you." He gave her a weak smile.

"Want to talk about it?"

Max hesitated before looking at her. "I think I want to file for temporary guardianship of Brinkley." He held her gaze, wondering what she might say.

"Really?" she asked.

"What rights do I really have right now? We take care of her, and we pay for anything she needs. Eventually something is going to come up, and being her brother is not going to be enough. What if we wanted to travel? What if my dad never actually comes home?"

"Have you talked to your dad about this?"

"I don't really care what he has to say. He abandoned his kids and ran off. He has postponed coming home month after month without any remorse or intention to come back."

"What about Rani? Are you going to do the same with her?"

"I don't know. She's old enough to make her own decisions. Brinkley is young."

"Are you prepared for how your dad might react?"

"What do you mean?" He got up and started pacing.

"What if you do this and then he comes back and takes both kids, and you're not in their life at all?" He stopped pacing and looked at her. "Loads them on a plane and flies off with them."

"Why didn't he do that to begin with?"

"Maybe because he was grieving still, and he thought he left them in good hands here so he could figure out his life."

"You're joking right?" He didn't want to fight with her over this. He thought she would be on his side.

"Can I give you an example and you won't get pissed at me?" He didn't respond. "What your dad did, leaving his kids with us, it's not that much different than you leaving Baer with me and going to Africa."

"Forget it," he said, hating the comparison but suddenly realizing the truth behind it. Like father, like son, he had abandoned his family with no real return date. He postponed coming home. He left it all open-ended, and Jules picked up the pieces. For his whole family.

"Max," she said, standing up and laying a hand on his arm.

"No. Forget I said anything," he told her, brushing her off and walking away. That was not how he thought that conversation would go. He could already see the vision of their happy little family, Jules being there with him and the kids in the cottage. Baer and Brinkley and Rani with them.

But he was just living in a dream world thinking that suddenly Jules would want to be that happy family with him again. At what point did he start picturing his future with Jules and not with Dani, or anyone else for that matter. Was that the answer he'd been looking for this whole time?

"I HAVE A COUPLE PASS-ONS," JULES SAID, WALKING UP TO Meg at the desk where she was discussing a patient with Max.

"Give them to Hudson."

"He's off in an hour," Jules returned.

"I'm covering her half shift," Max said casually, holding out his hand for the charts.

"Okay," she dragged out with question. She gave a rundown of five patients as she went over each chart, and Max made notes.

"Anything else?" he asked.

"Yeah. Do you have a second?"

"About a patient?" Max asked, looking up at her.

"No."

"Then, no," he said, before picking up the charts and turning to walk off.

Jules, head held high, turned in the opposite direction toward the lounge like that encounter was normal. Meg looked to Alex then saw Marco and Dani standing nearby, all of them having witnessed the clipped exchange.

"What was that about?" Marco asked, cornering Max before his shift ended.

"What?"

"You and Jules. Trouble in paradise?"

"Who am I kidding? It was a farce, remember. There was no paradise," Max commented, leaning back in his chair.

"That's bullshit. Never, in all the years I've known you, and all the years you've known Jules, have you ever had a conversation like that one. You've never even had a decent fight."

"Don't read too much into it. I had a lot of patients."

"And why the sudden need to pull an extra shift? Because you don't need the money."

"Meg asked me to cover. Hot date, I think?" Max pointed out as Dani walked up. "It's the least I could do for being an asshole years ago. And it's only a few hours."

"You're not getting off that easy," Marco said.

"Yes, I am," Max said with a smile. "What's up?" he asked Dani.

"Second opinion on my patient in three?" she asked.

"You got it."

He grabbed the stack of charts he was working on and followed her without another word to Marco. His spidey sense was telling him something was up with Marco, and he was deflecting to Max's trouble with Jules. The double date, spending more time in the ER, Meg's sudden requests for shift coverage for dates, and Marco pushing him toward Jules and Dani. He would normally group Meg into the list for a trifecta.

"Everything okay?" Dani asked when they came out of the room ten minutes later.

"Yeah. You?"

"Yeah." He didn't say anything as they walked back toward the desk. "Just seemed a little tense earlier with Jules."

"Everything's fine. Parenting stuff," he said, brushing it off. If he thought too much about how closely she related him to his father, it made him sick to his stomach. His whole adulthood he'd been doing everything possible to not become his father. To be his own person.

"Max, we're friends right?"

"Of course." Although they had barely talked since the birthday party, and there had not been another invite that put them alone together since.

"Then you know you can talk to me about anything."

"I appreciate the offer, but not when it comes to this."

"How come?" she asked, honestly.

"Because I don't want to hurt you. I need to figure some things out first."

"You mean figuring out you and Jules," she said, stopping in the middle of the hall. He slowed next to her and turned.

"I mean with my life."

"I guess I got the impression that you had a lot of that figured out after our recent discussion."

"It's complicated with kids involved."

"Kids," she repeated.

"My sisters. My dad being gone. My rights as a brother only. Things."

"Right," she said before starting to walk off.

"Dani," he said.

"Don't worry about it," she said.

Now he'd proceeded to piss off two women. He should just go for broke and add Meg to the mix. If only Meg wasn't off on her hot date tonight.

Six hours later, he went home alone for the first time since he could remember. To his big empty house, with lots of empty rooms, just next door to the house that held his heart.

The more this tore at him, the more he realized what he wanted, and what he wanted was Jules and their family. He was just doing a supreme job at ruining it all. They were lucky they made it this far without some major blow out. Is that because it was always so casual, and they didn't set the intention to be together forever?

He texted her late at night and let her know that Rosie was on deck to watch the kids if she wanted to drop them at the main house on her way into work. He should have guessed she would see his car and know he was home, too.

But instead of trying to talk to him, to wake him up, she left him alone.

She didn't text back.

20

JULY 2019

It had been all quiet on the western front for nearly a month. Without another word of discussion, Max dropped the idea of filing for temporary guardianship of Brinkley, at least vocally in front of Jules. He was still bouncing emails back and forth with his attorney trying to determine if, or when, they should pursue this avenue.

He also had not heard from his father since.

It was the height of summer, and all kids were bound and determined to spend every ounce of time possible outside. Rani had a budding boyfriend who spent a good deal of time at the house. The *twins* were loving their part-time nanny who also served as a child life specialist, which meant that even when they didn't think they were in school, they were still learning and were both reading above level. Sometimes it felt like they were smarter than the adults.

Max and Jules were still struggling, and it was mainly his fault. He felt like he was hiding from her, and she stopped fighting to get him to open up. Some days it was like Mad

Max had resurfaced, while other days he threw on a cloak of charm that no one could escape.

It doesn't mean there hadn't been heated moments when Max tried to ignore all the feelings and went with his basic animal instincts, and they still ended up naked together. She would wake up and he would be gone, and they wouldn't talk about it.

Today would be the double sucker punch. Jules had "plans" that night, which in Jules' speak sounded more like she had a date. Casually in passing at work as their shifts overlapped for five minutes, she asked if Rani was okay watching the kids in the evening for a few hours so she could go out.

"Fine," he said, before walking off.

***

HIS PHONE ALARM RANG ON THE NIGHTSTAND, AND HE fumbled to shut it off. He didn't even know what time he finally fell asleep after lunch when the kids were safely occupied with Rachel, their new nanny, and he could sneak away.

He gave her permission to allow the kids to come jump on the bed and wake him up if he wasn't downstairs by 5:30 p.m. to hear about their day and be part of dinner.

That probably means he only got about three hours of sleep. Perfect for a night shift.

Fresh out of the shower, he pulled a t-shirt over his head and opened the bedroom door to quiet, which was definitely not normal. Even in the big house, some sound echoed, TV, laughter, something.

When he hit the landing, he knew something was off. A stack of suitcases was piled inside the front door.

He detoured through the kitchen and poured a cup of

coffee, thanking the heavens for small mercies like Rosie and Rachel who kept him caffeinated and on schedule. He glanced out the window and saw the kids running around and Rachel sitting in a chair next to their guest - his father.

"Well, isn't this cozy," Max said, opening the back door and walking out onto the deck.

"Daddy," Baer yelled, and both kids ran toward him, latching onto his legs like they hadn't seen him in days. Max held the hot mug of coffee over his head until they had been appeased and sent them back to playing.

"I didn't want to wake you," Rachel said.

"It's okay," Max said. "I just wanted to have some time before dinner."

"I can take care of dinner," his father said. Max looked at him before glancing back at Rachel.

"I'm going to see what Rosie has up her sleeve. Be right back," she said, making her own disappearing act.

"Welcome back," Max said, watching the kids run and play.

"We took a red eye. I tried to call but service sucked."

"We?" He looked over at his father. "You brought her back with you?"

"Max, I was hoping this would be a positive thing. I finished up that big contract and now I'm home."

"It's great. Just a little more notice would have been nice. We have a pretty good schedule in place."

"Where is Jules?"

"She's at work until seven. I'm on night shifts."

"Is that healthy for your relationship?"

"What are you talking about?"

"If you're working opposite shifts, then when do you see each other?" Was his father purposely pointing out the flaws in the situation?

"It's temporary. Now that we have Rachel, I switch back to days."

"She's very sweet, and the kids seem to really like her."

"What's your plan, Dad?" Max asked. He didn't want to be playing this game. There was plenty of time to talk about Rachel and the kids. He needed to know about the immediate future.

"I'm home now. That should take some of the pressure off you. You can focus on your own family, and I will take care of mine."

"Baer and Brinkley are used to spending all day and night together."

"I'm sure they will still see each other plenty. She's his aunt." He said it like they were some close family that did Sunday brunch and picnics in the park and a big Christmas celebration. Like it wasn't weird to have an aunt your same age.

"And you're going to live at the house?"

"Why wouldn't I? I was surprised to find out you were here and not at the cottage."

"I stay at both depending on the schedule."

"Well, now you can enjoy staying in your own house."

Max could feel his blood pressure rising. He wasn't about to give his father the satisfaction of arguing about the real owner of the house yet again. He wasn't even sure his father remembered his Grami giving Max the house in her will, let alone his divorce from Jules over a year ago.

"I have to get ready for work. I'll see if Rachel can stay with Baer at the cottage until Jules gets home."

"Nonsense. He can stay with us."

"Great. Thanks." Max glanced over at the kids one last time before heading inside and running into Rachel in the kitchen.

"Everything okay?"

"Yeah. We might have a little change of plans now that my dad is home. Why don't you meet me at the cottage tomorrow instead of here?"

"Sounds good."

"He said he has the rest of the night covered, so why don't you escape while you can. Let him fend for himself."

She smiled. "Have a good shift."

He took the stairs two at a time and finished getting ready. He wanted to be out of there as soon as possible. He had ten hours to figure out how to crawl back to the cottage with his tail between his legs.

HE WOULDN'T NEED TO WALLOW TOO LONG IN HIS MIXED emotions at how things were playing out because the night shift left him too busy to think. It had to be a full moon or the apocalypse because everyone was coming out of the woodwork in the middle of the night.

"Hudson, call on line one."

"Take a message." His hair and scrub top were still soaked from the automatic fire sprinkler set off by some teenager high on mushrooms. His sneakers squeaked when we walked up to the board.

"It's Jules," David, the night clerk, said, holding out the phone. Max wrote a couple notes on the board.

"Unless someone is bleeding or dying, I'm not taking phone calls. I haven't even had a chance to change," Max told him before grabbing another chart and walking off.

"Did you catch that?" David said into the phone before hanging up.

"Why are you avoiding Jules?" Meg asked, walking up.

"I'm not avoiding Jules."

"Bad liar."

He stopped and turned to her, crossing his arms. "We have actual patients that we need to see. Let's get this over quickly."

"A month ago, you two were joined at the hip. It was disgusting. Now you avoid her calls. Trouble in paradise?"

He rolled his eyes. Trouble in paradise. The exact words Marco used not too long ago. Interesting.

"Who said it was ever paradise? Relationships are hard. Friendships are hard. They go through phases. Nothing is wrong. I just don't have time for a phone call to hear how her date went."

"Ah," she said with a smile.

"What?"

"You're jealous."

"Why would I be jealous?" He avoided eye contact.

"Because Jules is moving on, and you're getting nowhere with Dani." He scoffed.

"You definitely have no idea what you are talking about."

"It's like you're going through a midlife crisis, but you can't see it." She grinned. "Are you getting the sports car next?"

"Is this conversation over?" Max asked, uncrossing his arms.

"If you want Jules, like really, really want Jules, you need to man up and make a decision quickly. Because she's a catch, and your sorry ass is ruining it all."

"Thanks for the pep talk, Meg," he said before pushing open the exam room door and disappearing with a patient.

Six hours later, he didn't even remember his eyes closing when he took advantage of an empty exam room just to rest for a second before driving home.

"How was the night?" Jules asked, walking up to the desk at seven a.m.

"On a scale from one to chaotic, I would say full moon," Meg said, clearing off the last name on the board. "But we are leaving you with just the few new patients in the waiting room."

"No pass-ons?"

"Nope."

"Wow. I feel honored. I wish I could promise you the same." She wrote her name down and clocked in. "Is Max still here?"

"I think he's back in sutures," Meg said with a smile.

"Thanks." Jules dropped her stuff in the lounge, poured two cups of coffee and headed down the hall. He was going to talk to her whether he liked it or not. She pushed open the door with her elbow and was soaked in darkness, the only light from a suture lamp in the corner. Max was passed out cold, face down on the gurney.

She set the mugs on the nearest stand and slid over a stool, slowly sitting down before brushing the hair out of his face.

Doctors were never heavy sleepers, unless they pulled back-to-back all-nighters, and then it was like trying to rouse a vampire in daytime.

He stirred immediately and slowly opened his eyes to look at her.

"Hi," he whispered.

"Hi," she said back. "Nice job last night."

"No big shake," he said.

"Hence why you couldn't take my calls." He didn't say anything as he rolled over then sat up, running his hands through his hair. "Coffee?"

He took it willingly, and after breathing in the scent, took a sip.

"How was your date?"

"It wasn't a date." His eyebrow raised. "Drinks with an old colleague who was in town. He is thinking of transferring and wanted to get the scoop."

"If you say so."

She would let it go for now. "Why didn't you tell me your dad was back?"

"It just didn't come up."

"Okay. Then how about this, how long are you going to be acting this way, so I can put on my suit of armor to keep putting up with the BS you feed me day in and day out."

She was trying to play with him, she smiled a bit, but he couldn't even muster the strength to give it back. "I'm exhausted, Jules. I really don't want to do this right now."

"Then tell me when a good time is, because we work opposite shifts every single day and I barely see you in passing. I don't remember the last time we actually had a conversation of substance. I miss you, and I'm not letting you leave this room until this issue is taken care of." She waved a hand between the two of them.

"I'm just going through some stuff." He knew it was a lame excuse.

"Max, talk to me, please," she said, setting down her cup of coffee and laying a hand on the side of each knee.

"It's something I need to figure out for myself. Until I know, there's not really a point in talking about it."

"What do you mean?" He just looked at her. "Is this about Dani?"

"Partly."

"What's the other part? Brinkley and wanting custody?"

"No. Nothing with the kids, granted having my dad back is throwing me for a loop." He took a drink.

"Did something happen with Dani?"

"I can't talk about this with you."

"Why? You've never had a problem talking about her before."

"Things change." He stood up, and her hands fell from his legs. If she asked if it had to do with her, he would probably confess everything he'd been mulling over in his mind. Dani was just another casualty to his decision.

"Can we at least talk about our son and how your dad being back in town changes things?"

"You'll have to ask my dad what his plan is. I don't really expect him to stick with our routine."

"Well, we might need to finesse said routine since I had to leave home before you got there. Baer is at the main house. Why did you sleep here?"

"It was an accident. I thought I would close my eyes for five minutes before the next trauma. Didn't expect to sleep a couple hours. And I'm making some adjustments to my schedule," he said. He wanted out of that room and out of the conversation. He stepped toward the door, and she blocked him.

"We're in this together. We can both make adjustments, and we can both make sacrifices."

"Just let me take care of it," he said. "Let me take care of both of you."

"Who's going to take care of you?" she asked.

"I'm fine," he said. He looked at her, and she held his stare. She was daring him, calling his bluff, using Jedi mind tricks to get him to confess some secret. He could feel that stare down coarse through his belly to his toes. She was playing dirty.

At that moment, he didn't care if anyone saw them through the door, he didn't care if anyone walked in, he just didn't care. He was doing a really good job of not caring or pretending not to care.

So, he did the only thing he could think of to get her to leave him alone and stop talking.

He kissed her.

Not a polite first date on the doorstep kiss.

Not a cordial kiss on the cheek.

Not a sensual kiss good night.

Not a peck or sweep or sloppy plant.

He kissed her like there was no tomorrow. Every part of their bodies—toes, torso, chest, lips—touched as he pushed her up against the door, coffee cup still in hand. He didn't even give her a moment to adjust before his tongue swept over her lips and sunk in. He caressed her. His tongue made love to her mouth, reminding her of all the other places it had expertly made her knees go weak.

He pressed his hips into her and moaned deep, and her hands tangled in his hair and pulled him closer. He kept his hands to himself, putting all his energy on what his mouth could do.

Finally, he pulled back and took a step away from her. Her hands fell from his hair and a chill ran over his body at the sudden lack of contact.

"Max," she whispered.

"I don't know what I want. I don't know what I'm doing. But I think it might kill me if you decide to date someone else."

He didn't wait for a response; he didn't wait for her to stop him. He found the door handle, pulled open the exam room door, and left her in the dark.

Jules leaned back against the door after he left, a hand to her thoroughly kissed lips.

Oh, fuck, she thought.

21

PRESENT DAY

Max took a deep breath and tried to let a wave of calmness envelope him as he pulled up outside the main house. He would need to sleep soon but first he had to face his family, a.k.a. his father. He left the car in the drive and took the stairs two at a time before pulling open the front door.

Classical music was wafting through the house, the smell of breakfast similar to those he had in France or Italy, the windows were open letting in a light summer breeze.

No suitcases. No clutter. No sign of children. No sign of life.

Rachel had texted saying they were at the main house only ten minutes before, so he knew they were hiding somewhere, but he wasn't used to the lack of greeting.

Suddenly, like they couldn't resist any longer, the soft giggles erupted from the top of the stairs. Max looked up and found Baer, Brinkley, and Rachel looking through the railings down at him.

"Gotcha," Max said before rushing up the stairs to come

skidding behind them on the floor. "Tell me everything I missed," he said, laying down next to them, the kids taking a perch on each thigh and starting to talk in sync over each other.

Max smiled. Two children. Born so close together. Different parents. But without knowing any better, the perfect example of twins.

"Okay, okay," Rachel said. "How about we let Dad catch up a bit? Here's the parental recap. I just got here an hour ago, not much to report."

He laughed.

"If all goes well, we have a full day of catching toads, working on our spelling and reading, having a cooking lesson at lunch, quiet time, then hopefully afternoon snack with Dad. Does that sound good?" she asked the kids.

A chorus of *yeahs* echoed through the halls.

"Max," he heard his dad call. "Are you here?"

"Yeah, Dad."

"Oh, good. Come down to my study so we can talk."

"I just got off shift. I want to spend some time with the Doublemint Twins, then I need to crash."

"It will only take a minute."

Max sighed.

"Okay, rugrats. I need to do some adult discussion. You be good for Rachel. I'll see you in a few hours," Max said, pulling them both into a big hug and kiss.

He finally managed to get back to standing as the kids ran off to their room.

"I'm going to sleep at the cottage. Ringer is on. Call, text, whatever, if you need me. If my dad gets weird and wants to be only with Brinkley, you and Baer can hide out with me. Please don't just up and quit on me." He pressed both palms together in prayer.

"I promise," she said.

"Thanks." He gave her a soft smile before slowly walking back down the stairs like a scorned teenager about to be on house arrest.

"P.S., there's coffee in the kitchen," she said.

"You're my hero."

Max made a pit stop in the kitchen to find Rosie cooking. She didn't even ask as she grabbed a cup, poured in the black sludge, and handed it over.

"How bad?" he whispered.

"If I quit, will you hire me?" she asked.

"Of course," he said with a smile before walking out the opposite door and down the hall to his father's study. The one room he barely entered the whole time his dad was gone.

He knocked because that was what all polite rich boys were taught at a young age, but didn't wait for a response before opening the door and walking in.

"You beckoned," Max said casually, leaving the door open. It smelled musty, much like it had been closed up for the better part of a year.

"I just wanted to make sure we are all on the same page."

"With what?" Max asked.

"Well, I know you and Jules have a way of doing things, but I think it's best if I set a new routine with Brinkley and Rani now that I'm back."

"Of course," Max said. Maybe the less he said, the sooner he would get out of there.

"I will need to start going back into the office next week, board meetings, etc. I think we would both agree that Brinkley and Baer would be lonely if they were apart, and she seems to love Rachel."

"Agreed."

"It might be best if they do their school work at your

house during the day and then be at their separate homes at night. I'm looking into private schools for Brinkley. Have you chosen a school for Baer?"

"Challenger. Both kids are enrolled. If you disagree, give them a call and make other arrangements. Rachel will be staying on for after school care until one of us gets home."

"Great. I noticed you still have quite a bit of stuff in your old bedroom."

"I'll take care of it," Max said.

"Perfect. I know we'll still be seeing each other around, but I want the kids to get back to understanding I am their father and will take care of them."

"Certainly. Is there anything else?" Max asked, taking a sip of his coffee. Years of random schedules and all-nighters meant caffeine and coffee really did nothing to mess with his sleep, or energy. It was a comfort, not a necessity. Anything to distract him from the pain of his father taking back responsibility, pulling Rani and Brinkley away from him, staking his rightful claim.

"John, I think I just found the perfect villa to take the kids to this summer," a voice said, interrupting them. Max froze. "I'm sorry. I didn't realize you were in a meeting."

"We're done," John said with a wave. Max gritted his teeth. His father was treating him like a business meeting, not his son. "Have Rachel bring Brinkley back around five tonight for dinner."

Max took a deep breath before turning around and coming face to face with Carrie. His Carrie. Now his dad's Carrie, who also seemed one second away from being his stepmother.

"Max," she said.

"That's right. You two haven't met."

"Oh, we have," Max said, coldly.

"Great. Saves me time," he turned back to his work, leaving them standing there in silence.

Max shook his head then left the room. He set his mug on a random table and headed for the stairs. He knew she followed but hoped she would keep her distance. He definitely wasn't in the mood.

"Hey, Rachel," he said softly, poking his head into the room, then motioned for her to come out.

"What's up?" she asked.

"New change of plans. You're going to hang with the kids at the cottage during the day."

"Okay."

"And I need to vacate the premises. I'm going to pack up a bunch of clothes now from my room, but can you discretely pack up Baer's stuff from here and move it back to Jules'?"

"Of course."

"Thanks."

He disappeared into his room down the hall, and she caught a glance of him as he headed back down the stairs carrying two duffle bags.

"I don't want to talk to you," Max said when he found Carrie waiting in the foyer.

"I'm the one who should be mad, not you," she said.

"Explain that one to me? Because I'm pretty sure it looks like you're shacked up with my father," he hissed, opening the front door. She followed him out.

"I didn't know he was your father when I met him, but now that I know it makes sense why I was drawn to him. And for the record, you left me high and dry."

"Spare me," he said, tossing the two bags into the back of the Range Rover. He could wait to come back for the next load.

"It's not like I planned this. I didn't know anything about

your life. You didn't talk about home, kids, wife..." she trailed off.

"I'm not married."

"Your dad certainly thinks you are."

"Good for him." He opened the driver's door, and she stopped him. "Let go."

"I don't want this to be weird."

"We're well past that. It wasn't that long ago you were calling me, crying, upset that I left you all alone there. Now, here you are living the high life."

"Max."

"I think it's best that you just keep your distance for a while. I have enough shit going on."

"I'll talk to him. He doesn't need to kick you out of his house."

Max laughed. *His house.* "Legally, it's my house," he told her before finally managing to close the driver's door. She still had a lot to learn.

She watched him drive away.

He woke up suddenly. It had been a long time since he'd had a nightmare, but seeing Carrie was bringing back memories of Africa, and that brought back pain. He knew it was in his head, but it still felt so real, reliving the pain of the bullets, the blunt force trauma that nearly stopped his heart, unable to breath.

His shirt was drenched through, and the sheets were a mess.

Taking a deep breath, he finally crawled out of bed and headed for the shower. He didn't know how long he had been standing under the hot spray letting it beat down on his skin and wash away the memories, but he felt the air in the room shift.

Turning his head to the glass shower door, he saw Jules leaning against the counter with a glass of wine, ankles crossed, just watching him.

"Turning into a voyeur now, are we?" he asked.

"Just wondering if I should call the cops because I found a man in my shower and two wily children in my living room."

"You're home early," he commented.

"It was quiet. Dani offered to cover my last hours. Why are you here?" She said playfully with a smile.

"We got our eviction notice from the main house."

"What do you mean?" she asked, her playful tone disappearing.

"My father would like MY house all to himself, HIS children, and his NEW girlfriend."

"Which one of those are you really upset about?"

"What do you mean?"

"Are you angry because a: your father is back; b: he's commandeered your house as his own, effectively forcing you to move back in with me; c: he is laying claim to his children who you have been caring for; or d: his girlfriend?"

"They are all equal on scale."

"That's not true."

He set to work washing his hair, washing his body, all while he talked.

"It's good he's back. It takes the pressure off us to take care of three kids. I can barely take care of myself, so really it's taking a lot of pressure off you."

"Don't make excuses for me. Continue."

"I don't care about the house, but the proper thing would

be to acknowledge he doesn't actually own it and be grateful I don't kick him to the curb. Or sell it."

"Your grandmother would not approve."

"He can afford his own place."

"Which would end up being farther away from you, putting distance between Baer and Brinkley and you and Rani. It's convenient being next door." He shut off the shower and grabbed the nearest towel. He came out with it wrapped around his waist, but the rest of his body still glistened with water.

"So, it must be option d. The girlfriend."

"Did you meet her?"

"No. Is she that terrible?"

Max didn't respond, choosing instead to step closer to her, taking the glass of wine out of her hand and taking a drink before handing it back and leaning closer to her, putting his hands on the counter on either side of her.

"Jules."

"Max."

"I have to go to work," he said before giving her a quick peck and stepping into the closet.

"Rip off the bandaid," she said.

"What?" he questioned.

"Just get it all out in the open and off your chest. You'll feel a lot better."

"Are we still talking about my dad?"

"Sure," she said. She would welcome anything he wanted to talk about as long as he kept talking. The silence between them over the past couple weeks had been tough. She missed her best friend. She missed him.

"It's Carrie," he said, coming back out carrying his shoes.

"Who?"

"My dad's girlfriend is Carrie. From Africa."

When he left for Africa, he was newly divorced and struggling with the emotions and feelings about Jules and their failed relationship. Months after Carrie entered his life, he told Jules about her, about how he had met another doctor, how she was different but nice, that he didn't have strong feelings about her, but something happened. He didn't want to keep her a secret. He knew Jules deserved better. He equated it to another Meg, with red hair.

He still considered Jules his best friend. He was used to telling her everything. He knew he probably hurt her, but she stayed strong, she told him she understood, and it was okay. They were divorced.

And when he came home, he told Jules the rest, how he was stupid for using Carrie just to fill a void. He tried to avoid her, and when he got hurt, he left without a word. He hurt her just like he hurt Meg. A vicious cycle. Except the whole time he was with Carrie all he thought about was Jules.

"You're joking, right?" She brought him back to the present.

"I wish." He actually wanted to laugh but instead walked out of the room and was already halfway down the stairs before she caught up with him.

"When did that happen?" she asked.

"Don't know, don't care."

He sat on the bench at the entry and started tying his shoes. He could hear Baer giggling in the room next to them.

"Max, you can't be serious."

"Why would I even joke about something like this?" He stood and walked into the living room. "Alright Baer boy, I have to go to work. Be good for Mom. Eat all your veggies. Go to bed early."

"Yes, Daddy," he said, holding out his arms. Max picked

him up and squeezed him, kissed the top of his head, and tossed him back onto the couch.

"You don't have to be at work yet."

"You're here. I'm ready." He shrugged.

"You're avoiding. I think you should get off constant night shifts," she told him before he could get out the front door. He was checking his pockets to make sure he had everything.

"Why?"

"Well, we have Rachel, and if you're sleeping all day, then it's not like you're with Baer."

"I'll try not to take that as a negative."

"It's not."

"Okay, I'll think about it." He didn't tell her it was already in progress. He didn't tell her how much he missed her. He didn't tell her he would do anything she asked of him.

"If we had the same shifts, we'd actually get to spend time together as a family."

He opened the front door and looked at her. What was she really saying?

"Rip off the bandaid," Max said with a smile before slipping on his sunglasses.

"I don't think I want you dating other people either," she said. His grin widened at her, then without another word, he was out the door and in the car.

22

A FEW DAYS LATER

"Look who's back to the land of the living," Alex said as Jules and Max walked into the ER with their matching cups of coffee.

"You didn't think you got rid of me forever, did you?" Max asked.

Back to normal, he wrote both their names on the board and jogged to catch back up to Jules heading for the lounge. It had been a long week, mostly spent with Max sleeping as little as possible to spend time with his son, help everyone start adjusting to a new routine, and forcing himself to be more available and around with Jules. They shared the bed and the bedroom but only once had they both been in it together.

"What did you tell your dad?" she asked him.

"About what?"

"Dinner."

"I told him no." He held the door open for her.

"Thanks. But why?"

"Because I don't want to have dinner with them. It's as

simple as that."

"He's your father."

"And she's his girlfriend. Simple as that."

"You always know what kind of day it's going to be depending on if Jules and Hudson are fighting," Bobby said.

"We're not fighting," they both said before opening their own lockers.

"Rounds start in thirty seconds," Maine yelled through the closed door.

Their lockers closed with a collective thud. Max grabbed his coffee cup and held the door open for her again. "Ladies first." He purposely walked through before Bobby giving him a Cheshire grin.

"It might not be as bad as you think," Jules said.

"It's usually worse."

"What about the sleepover?" Jules asked as they walked up to the admit desk where everyone was gathering.

"Brinkley can come over and spend the night at our house, but I'm not sending our son to their house overnight."

"Don't you think you're overreacting a bit."

"Don't you think maybe we should talk about this at home?" he asked quietly.

"Are you two, like, back together?" Bobby asked loudly enough to get the attention of the whole room.

Max turned to look at him but didn't respond. Jules took a sip of her coffee.

"When did you break up?" Kelley commented.

"He went to Africa. Enough said," Bobby interjected.

"Enough said, indeed," Maine said. "How about we do some work? Who's starting?"

Max kept his mouth shut, taking the charts handed to him. Jules did the same. It didn't go unnoticed that Dani kept a close eye on both of them, and Max didn't miss the smirk that Meg was sending his way.

He glanced at her and took a sip of coffee, casually giving her his middle finger with a smile back. Meg just shook her head.

He found it interesting that there was a good possibility no one knew they had even got divorced. And knowing his colleagues there was probably a betting pool on that fact already.

"Alright, if there isn't anything else," Maine said. "Get to work."

Max wanted to turn to Jules and comment, not caring what other people thought but hesitant to bring any more attention to them. They were back to their casual, easy going way. Both of them simply stating they didn't like the other one dating was all it took to bring them closer together again.

"Hudson," Maine said before he could disappear with his charts.

"Yes, ma'am."

"Walk with me." He fell into step beside her down the hall with his coffee and charts.

"Where are we going?"

"Just for a walk."

"Okay," he said.

"I'm going to ignore that little personal display earlier."

"I had nothing to do with that."

"I don't care. Just try to keep your personal life, or drama, out of the ER."

"Of course. Is that all?" She was heading up the stairs, and he stopped. She motioned him to keep walking.

"There are some changes coming. Have you thought about applying for the Chief of Emergency Medicine position?"

"I wasn't aware of an opening to apply for."

"Just a little heads-up. I know you're still adjusting and working out some personal things in your life, but a lot of the doctors and staff look up to you. I think you would be a great leader."

"I appreciate the vote of confidence, but I don't know if I'm the right guy for the job."

"Why do you say that?"

"I'm not great with deadlines, I'm not a meeting person, I avoid the hard stuff. I really just want to practice medicine then go home and be with my family."

"I am happy to disagree with you. While there may be a little bit of extra learning and some reports and meetings, you would be running the ER the way you feel is best. Delegate the stuff you don't like to someone else."

"Have you talked to Jules about this?"

"Why would I talk to Jules about you applying for the position?"

"About her applying for the position. We're both senior attendings. She is definitely more responsible and qualified."

"I mentioned it to her. Do I need to worry about a conflict of interest, jealousy, fighting, and undercutting authority?"

"With Jules?" he half laughed.

"You think I don't notice everything, but I do. It's been pretty tense between you two. If you both apply, we can only promote one of you, so if there are going to be any issues professionally or personally, get them resolved before the decision is made."

"There won't be issues."

"Good. On a personal note, and as your friend, how is everything going?" she asked.

"Fine."

"Man of few words."

"Like you said, working on some things."

"Alright then. Get to work," she said before leaving him standing in the hall. *That was interesting*. His phone buzzed, and he took it out of his pocket. Text from Rani.

"This is torture. Can I please just move in with you? Are you living with Jules? Ugh!" Then she proceeded to use every annoying and upsetting emoji she could.

He smiled.

"Naughty text?" Marco said, sneaking up next to him.

"Opposite. My sister. Teenage drama. She's stuck living with our dad now that he's back, and apparently it isn't going so well."

"Sometimes I wouldn't mind having that simple drama back in my life."

"Really? Try having a kid sister half your age."

"What time is your shift over?" Marco asked as they headed back downstairs to the ER.

"Seven."

"Drinks, dinner, and dancing?"

"Are you propositioning me?" Max asked.

"You wish. Bring someone. Jules, Dani, whoever."

"What makes you think I want to bring anyone anywhere right now?"

"These walls have ears. Still haven't made a decision?"

"I made a decision. I just don't know if I'm ready for you to get up in my business again."

"That's what friends are for."

"Who are you bringing?" Max asked, as they made it back to the admit desk.

"It's a surprise."

"How do you know it's not the same person I would bring?"

"It's not."

"How do you know?"

"Trust me."

"The two most dangerous words out of your mouth." Max wrote his name on the board under his charts.

"Max, do you have a second?" Dani asked, walking up.

"One minute. I need a refill." He didn't wait for either of them to pipe up before making a quick jog down the hall to the lounge.

He pushed open the door to find Meg shutting her locker and gathering up her stuff. He quickly refilled his cup and without a word headed out the door. She was hot on his heels.

"So, no more rocky road to romance?" she asked with a smile.

"You remind me of my kid sister. Just more annoying."

"I'll take that as a compliment because I know how much you love Rani."

"I have nothing to say," Max said.

"If you and Jules are making it work, then I'm happy for you." He didn't comment. "If you're moving on to some other girl, like maybe Dani, just do Jules a favor and don't let her find out about your nuptials in the paper."

"Well, thanks for that," he said sarcastically. "Now go away, I have to work," he said, turning the opposite direction of her, almost forgetting that Dani needed something. "Sorry," he said. "What'd you need?"

She hesitated. "It's nothing. I just wanted to pick your brain about something."

"What?" he asked in typical male fashion, not catching on to the fact that it wasn't at all work related and maybe having the conversation in front of their colleagues wasn't the best idea.

"I'll track you down later," she said.

He stood there watching her walk away then looked over at Marco who was just shaking his head. "Dude, you're clueless."

"What?" he asked, looking around.

"Yeah. Definitely clueless," Alex popped in.

"Well, is someone going to fill me in?"

"Not it," Alex said before going back to work.

"What are we arguing about?" Jules asked, walking up and crossing off two names. "Max, have you even seen a patient yet?"

"Not my fault you got all the discharges, and I have all the cases with five follow-up tests."

"Less whining, more treating patients."

Max saluted her and walked off.

"Wait, before you go. Jules, Max needs a hall pass tonight. Can you babysit?" Marco asked. Max grabbed the nearest piece of paper, crumpled it, and threw it at Marco.

"Babysit my own kid?" she asked. "I do it every night, why would tonight be any different?"

"Perfect. Thanks," Marco said before walking off.

"What was that about?" Jules turned and asked Max, but he was already entering an exam room.

23

PRESENT DAY

"Hey Max, your sister is on line two," Alex said, stopping him halfway to his next patient.

"Shit," Max said before taking the phone. "Hi, sorry. I got busy at work." He listened, jotting a few notes down on a couple charts before sticking them back on the rack. "I know. Did you tell him that? Did you ask him about moving in with me?"

He saw Dani walk up and looked at his watch. It had been five hours since she asked to talk to him. He covered the phone, "Give me a minute, and I'll meet you outside," he told her.

She nodded and walked off.

"No, I'm here. I'll talk to him, but I don't think he'll agree to it. Well, I need to talk to Jules, too." He smiled at her inquiry into his living arrangements. "No comment. Okay, fine. You babysit tonight and I promise to come over for dinner tomorrow, and I will talk to him." He held the phone away from his ear. "Okay, I have to go. I gotta go. Rani, no I don't want to talk to Carrie. I gotta go."

He didn't wait for another response and just hung up.

"Alex, I'm taking a break," he said before walking out of the waiting area. Dani was sitting on a bench, eyes closed, with her head back. "Hey," he said, sitting down next to her and bumping her knee with his knee.

"Hey."

"What's going on?" he asked casually, already having a pretty good idea.

"I feel a little silly bringing this up."

"Don't. I want to know what you're thinking."

"I told you that when I decided to come back, it wasn't with some fantasy hope that we could start where we left off."

"Right."

"I am glad that we're becoming friends again."

"Me, too."

"I just kind of need to know, for myself, if friends is all we're going to be."

Max looked down at his shoes. He knew this time would come, and he wished he was the one who had the guts to bring it up.

"When you left, I think it broke my heart," he told her. "But it's what you needed to do. Just like I had to go to Africa. The difference is, you were running toward something good. If you stayed for me, I probably would have always wondered if you would resent me for holding you back, or what if it never even worked out and you sacrificed the opportunity. When I left, I was running away, trying to escape. It wasn't healthy. Jules was an unexpected turn in my life, and I think she saved me. Twice."

"I really wish I knew how you felt back then."

"I was a coward. Hell, I still am. I couldn't be the one to bring up this conversation."

"I get the feeling you have a lot going on." It was an understatement.

"I've learned a lot about myself the past few months. I let my family down once already. I didn't know what the right answer was or the right choice. I was just so focused on putting my life back together every single day."

"And it led you back to Jules. It makes sense."

"Why do you say that?"

"You were married to her. You have a child together. It's safe to say you don't really fight. You're like the dream couple. The Hallmark card for families."

"That's taking it to an extreme."

"Max, maybe you can't see what the rest of us see, but what you have with Jules is the real deal. And I should have realized that the moment I came back."

"I'm really sorry," he said.

"Nothing to be sorry for."

"Friends."

"Always."

She took his outstretched hand with a smile.

24

THAT NIGHT

"I thought this was boys' night or something," Jules said as they navigated the streets of downtown Boise.

Max had made Jules patiently wait four hours before their shift was finally over to ask if she wanted to be his date to dinner with Marco. No better offers had shown up he told her, which got him a punch to the arm and a laugh.

"No. It's date night. Marco has this new girl, I guess. He wanted me to come out, meet her, and bring someone."

"So, this is like a coming out party?"

He reached over and took her hand but didn't say anything. After a moment he brought their hands up to his lips and kissed the back of her hand.

"Does he know who you're bringing?"

He shrugged. "Probably."

"Who is he bringing?" she asked.

"He didn't tell me, but I have an idea."

"Who?" she asked, squeezing his hand and turning slightly in her seat to look at him.

"Meg." He shot her a sideways glance then looked back at the road as he turned into the parking garage.

"Really?"

"It's just a feeling. I could be wrong. He kind of gets around. Hard to keep up."

"But if he's wanting to do date night, then it must be somewhat serious."

"I don't really know."

"Does she know who's coming to dinner?"

"I don't know." Jules rolled her eyes. Typical male not asking questions and just showing up, rolling with the punches.

He maneuvered into a parking spot and shut the car off. "Don't move," he said, before getting out of the car and coming around to her side and opening the door.

"What is this?" she asked, taking his hand and stepping out with a smile.

"Date night."

"We've never done this," she told him.

"What?"

"The wooing and chivalry." He closed the door and smiled down at her, cornering her with his arms against the car. "The dating."

"We went on dates," he told her.

"Not in the beginning."

"Of course, we did. We used to have daily coffee and lunch dates."

"As friends."

"It was more than friends to me," he whispered, kissing her cheek.

"If I remember correctly, you were dating someone else."

"Sleeping with someone else. Minor detail." He kissed her other cheek. "You're beautiful, you know," he said before kissing her leisurely. It reminded him of the first time he ever kissed her, a little hesitant of what she would do, more confident that she wouldn't push him away, and definitely one of the most natural things he'd ever done.

"We're going to be late," she whispered.

"I don't care." Finally, he relented and stepped back. "Okay. We can go now."

He held her hand on the elevator ride down three flights, opened the door to the street, and entwined their hands again for the short walk to the restaurant.

"I'm kind of surprised your dad didn't put up a fuss about Rani staying over tonight."

"I made him a deal."

"Oh really. This should be good," she said as he opened the door to Alavita.

"I told him we would have dinner at the main house tomorrow with them."

"We?" she asked.

"You don't expect me to go alone, do you?" He squeezed her hand, seeing Marco and Meg already seated at a table in the corner.

"You were right," she said.

"I like when you say that," he said, letting her walk ahead of him, a hand on the small of her back.

"Don't get used to it."

"Sorry we're late. Kids." Max said. He pulled out a chair for Jules then sat down across from Marco.

"Terrible excuse," Marco said.

"Fine. Jules couldn't decide what to wear." She rolled her eyes as the waiter came over to get their drink order.

"So," Max said with a smile, leaning back in his chair and casually draping an arm on the back of Jules' chair, his fingers brushing against her bare skin.

"So," Marco said with a smile back at him. They were right, and they knew it, both having guessed who they were each bringing as a date. Their "so" spoke volumes to each other. Their universal man language.

"You two are ridiculous," Jules said.

"I agree," Meg concurred. "I told Marco I didn't like keeping it a secret anymore. I didn't think you would have a problem with it considering..."

"Considering what?" Max asked.

"You're back with Jules. Obviously." Meg looked between the two of them, no feelings of hurt or resentment or jealousy came bubbling to the surface. She'd never seen them together outside of work. She was used to their banter and professional relationship but was surprised at the cool and calm Max Hudson that showed up when he was with Jules in public.

"Oh, this? We're just friends. My other hot date wasn't available," Max said with a wink.

"I don't know why I put up with you," Jules said as their wine arrived.

"Because you love me, and I'm cute," Max said. "How about a toast?"

"To what?" Marco asked.

"Friendship and the gorgeous women who put up with us," Max said. They clinked glasses.

"So, really, how long has this been going on?" Max asked, looking between Marco and Meg.

"I don't know. A while," Marco casually said.

"Since you were in Africa," Meg said at the same time.

"That's longer than a while. And you managed to keep it out of the hospital? No one can keep secrets there."

"What are you talking about? You're the master at ER secret-keeping," Meg countered.

"Do tell. I wouldn't mind a little Hudson gossip," Marco said.

"This doesn't sound like a fun game to me," Max said.

"Well, there was that one time when you switched the contents of everyone's lockers but kept their name tags," Meg said. "I don't know how you did it in thirty minutes with no one finding out."

"I had help," he said with a smile before looking at Jules.

"Don't drag me into this. I busted you, and you black-mailed me."

"Then there was the male stripper you ordered for Maine for her 40th birthday."

"She just broke up with her boyfriend. I wanted to cheer her up," Max defended.

"And, what about that anonymous donation for cancer research. In the amount of half a million."

"What?" Marco asked wide eyed.

"Anonymous for a reason," Max pointed out.

"And the parade of desperate housewives who brought their kids in with bee stings, tummy aches, and slivers, just so Prince Charming could help out, smile, and flirt with them. They weren't getting it at home, so they came to see Max."

"Is that why you always get a stack of mail on your birth-day?" Jules asked him.

"Well, I didn't want to give them my home address, and they all seemed like they needed someone to take care of," Max said innocently.

"I figured you would know all the juicy gossip," Meg said to Jules.

"Why? Just because I married him?"

"Or you were in on all his shenanigans," Meg pointed out.

"Once a year, maybe, I did something out of the ordinary. Not always," Max tried defending himself.

"Try once a week."

"You realize that Kelley and Bobby have their own share of stunts."

"They aren't clever enough to get away without anyone knowing though."

"Obviously, I'm not either if you seem to know them all."

"It's called a drunken confession," Jules pointed out.

Meg nodded. "It's true. It's a Max thing."

"I've met that Max," Marco said.

"When? My history only involves women trying to get me drunk to know all my secrets," Max said.

"Bachelor party."

"Whose?" Meg asked. "No one we know has gotten married since…"

They all looked at Marco, and he realized he gave up one secret they hadn't really ever shared. More like a lie by omission.

"What are you talking about?" Meg asked. "Are you talking about Max's bachelor party?"

This was a touchy subject, and it could go a couple of ways. If Meg was really okay with Max's relationship with Jules, if she was in love with Marco and over the shitty way Max treated her, then this conversation would be fine.

"I thought you eloped," Meg said to Max. "Marco didn't even start at the hospital until a couple years ago." Max took a drink of wine preparing himself to tell her the truth.

"I was dating one of Jules' friends. My girlfriend at the time was going on this getaway with her and some other friends, and she invited me. We didn't even talk about where we worked so it was a surprise later when I showed up at the hospital and they were both there." Marco gave one version of how they met.

"You're the reason I went on the trip," Max confessed. Maybe they could break the ice a bit and ease into it.

"Excuse me," Jules said with a smile.

"It was supposed to be a girls' trip, and then all the girls started inviting boys. You said you didn't want to be the only one going solo," Max said, smiling back.

"Wow," Meg said.

"We don't have to talk about this," Max said.

"No, it's okay. I'd rather we just get all this awkward past out in the open and never have to worry about it again."

Max looked at Marco then back and Meg.

"Jules knows everything. She had no problem telling me that I was the world's biggest asshole," Max said. "It's a title I still can't live down," he tried to joke.

"I know you two dated, but I guess I didn't think it was a big deal," Marco said. Obviously, Max hadn't given him the full run down. "Especially because when I met you, I would have guessed you and Jules had been together for years."

"As friends, yes. But I did not handle anything well back then. Hell, even now. I ran away from problems, and Meg had to find out about Jules and me from a newspaper announcement. I didn't have the courage to tell her."

"It's water under the bridge now," Meg said. She was done dwelling on her past with Max. Tonight was supposed to be about their futures.

"I know, but I'm still sorry."

"So, Jules was your big secret," Marco said.

"Pretty sure no one realized anything past friendship was going on with us until that wedding announcement," Jules said.

"That's some secret. How long were you actually dating

before you got married? Or should I not ask that?" Marco said, looking at Meg.

Max looked at Meg, asking for permission. She knew the answer, but it still didn't make hearing it out loud any easier.

"It's okay, Max. I'm okay," she told him, taking Marco's hand.

"A few months." Marco whistled. He was not expecting that answer.

"We'd been best friends for probably five years before anything ever happened," Jules said.

"Chalk it up to one night with a few too many glasses of wine and drunken confessions. What man could resist a beautiful woman?" Max said. "I'm actually surprised she didn't punch me and kick me out."

"I was in it for the money," Jules joked.

"I should have thought of that," Meg said with a smile. "Your grandmother hated me."

"She did not. She wasn't happy with me. My father wasn't happy with me. I was a screw up back then," Max said.

"Back then?" Jules countered.

"Point taken. And you still put up with me."

"At this rate, I don't think anyone else will take you," Jules said with a smile.

"Enough of this. Drink up, and let's gossip about those other jokers at work," Max said.

25

THE NEXT NIGHT

"Are you ready to go?" Jules asked, walking downstairs to find Max watching the stocks on TV with a highball glass in hand.

He was still adjusting to being back on days after living like a zombie for months, and a year in Africa with no set sleep schedule. Sometimes he had moments in the middle of a trauma where it felt like he was suddenly waking up. His brain had been on autopilot, and then something clicked, and he realized he was probably walking around unaware for hours. It was that same feeling he had when driving home, pulling in the garage, and realizing he couldn't remember a moment of the drive or how he got there.

Throughout his shift, he had been dreading this dinner with his father. The last family dinner they had, Justine was still alive. She'd just found out she had end-stage breast cancer, and treatments weren't working. His father got drunk, Justine went to bed early, Jules took Baer home for bed, and Max sat in his father's study and let him take out all his anger at cancer, his Grami's death, and his mother's death, on him.

He was a failure. He could never measure up. His mother would have wanted more for him. He was a shitty father. He was never around. He couldn't understand how someone as smart as Jules would marry him. They gave him all the luxuries in the world, and Max threw them in their face.

Max took it all with his head high, alcohol can make you tell the truth, it certainly did with Max. And when his father stopped rambling, Max put his own glass down, and with his hands in his pockets so he wouldn't be tempted to punch his own father, he said he never wanted to see him again.

"I could use another drink," he said before draining the glass and turning off the TV.

"You can have one there. Is that what you're wearing?" she asked, looking at his jeans and T-shirt.

"What's wrong with what I'm wearing? He's already going to be judging me."

"Putting on some slacks and a button up won't hurt anything."

"Are you going to help me change?" he asked with a wink.

"No."

"I liked Africa. No one cared what you smelled like, dressed like, looked like. You were lucky if people just showed up."

"Go change."

"I was going to change anyway," he told her, setting down his glass and walking to the stairs. He was buttoning a crisp white shirt when she joined him carrying his highball glass with a refill. She handed it to him then kissed him softly.

"We've had dinner with your dad plenty of times. This is not going to be that bad."

"I'm not looking forward to the *I told you so,* or what a

disappointment I am, or how being a doctor is not a good use of my time."

"He's never said that."

"Not when anyone else is around."

He never told her about the last time. She never asked why they hadn't been back since. Justine passed away not too long after, his father was in mourning and spent all his time working. Max and Jules helped take care of the girls. Max, like his father, held all the rejection inside, focused on work, and pretending he had the dream life. Until Jules mentioned separating. It was the final piece that broke him. He still kept that inside. He'd recovered from it because she helped put him back together without even realizing it.

"So, I won't let him be alone with you." She'd come up behind him with a suit jacket and held it out for him to slide in his arms.

"He can be very persuasive. Plus, there's this thing about the men going off together so they can smoke cigars and leaving the women in another room so they can gossip."

"You don't smoke cigars. Besides, you have an early shift tomorrow, so we can use that as an excuse to get out early. And Baer needs to go to bed at a decent time."

"This is why I keep you around. Home by nine."

"Sounds mighty fine." He turned around and kissed her. She smiled around his lips. He took that as permission and pulled her closer, angling his head slightly to deepen their connection, his teeth pulling gently on her lower lip.

"Max," she whispered.

"Ten minutes."

"Later."

"Now." Even though she didn't step away from him, she angled her head back and away from his lips.

"We're going. If you're a good boy, I'll give you a treat when we get home."

"What kind of treat?"

"It's a secret."

"Give me something to look forward to."

"I'm not wearing any panties," she whispered to him before fully stepping out of his grasp.

He groaned before picking up the glass and drinking the remaining contents. She was going to slowly kill him. As far as he knew, she'd only done it on two other occasions - not long after they first started dating and right after they got married. Both times she told him in the lounge when they started their shift. They almost got caught in exam rooms and dark corners while he tried to sneak a peek.

"If he brings up the divorce, just lie." He needed to take his mind off Jules naked and calm his body down a little bit.

"Why am I lying?"

"One less reason I'm a disappointment?" he suggested, slipping his feet into loafers and picking up his glass to walk downstairs.

"Are we also lying about your history with Carrie? Does he even know about that?"

"I don't know. I haven't said anything. Kind of feel like that's her deal."

"I'm not a fan of secrets," she said. "Not these kinds of secrets."

"I know. Just don't bring it up and maybe we'll be fine." He kissed her cheek before opening the front door. "I still don't want Baer having a slumber party over there either. Just because we're having dinner doesn't mean we're one big happy family," he said.

"Max," she groaned.

"Maybe we'll get called to the hospital for some big case."

"I left my phone at home."

"Cheater." They walked hand in hand through the hidden passageway and into the yard of the main house. Sometimes it still shocked Max that he owned that place or even that he was the lucky sucker who grew up there when it felt like he deserved to be in a shack.

The front door opened before they even made it up the steps, and Baer ran out.

"Daddy," he said, throwing himself at Max who threw him over his shoulder to carry him inside.

"Have you been a good boy?" Max asked.

"I'm always a good boy," he said.

"Hey," Carrie said at the top of the stairs holding Brinkley's hand. "I'm glad you decided to join us."

Brinkley immediately released her hand and started down the stairs and nearly launched herself at Max before she reached the bottom.

"Hey, Princess," he whispered.

"I missed you," she said.

"I know." With another squeeze, she was wiggling out of his arms into Jules'.

"Dinner is almost ready, but we have some appetizers in the den. Wine?" she asked.

"Sure," Max agreed as they all followed her like proper guests.

"Max," Rani called as he walked in and ran over to give him a hug.

"Someone's popular," Carrie joked with a soft smile to his father.

"You just saw me yesterday," he told her with a hug.

"Different than seeing you every day," she whispered just to him.

"We're figuring it out," he said.

"Tonight? Are you going to ask him?"

"Let's just see what happens." Carrie came over and handed them both a glass of wine.

"Max, Jules," his father said, walking over to shake his hand and kiss her cheek. "Glad we were finally able to make this work."

"We're happy to be here," Jules said. It almost felt like they were thrown back in time standing in this room, announcing they were married. Then again, when Jules was pregnant, an announcement that came shortly after his father's bombshell about Brinkley's pending arrival.

"I'm happy to see you two are back together," he said, taking a sip of his scotch. Of course his dad's interference would start immediately with no buffer.

"Excuse me?" Max questioned. He didn't miss all three women in the room looking at him.

"I just know marriage is hard, and you two had your share of rough patches."

"This isn't really dinner talk, Dad," Max said.

"You're right, I apologize," he said as Rosie walked into the room to announce dinner.

"Disaster," Max whispered to Jules. She kept silent even though her intuition was signaling distress. This might actually blow up in her face.

Baer and Brinkley demanded to sit next to each other, and Rani wanted to sit by Max, which left the two men at the heads of the table.

"We're thinking of heading to St. Barts for a month. Take the kids," his father said after a prolonged silence.

"That will be nice," Jules said with a smile.

"Dad," Rani said hesitantly, glancing at Max.

"What, sweetheart?"

"Can I stay here? With Max?" she asked. His hands

stilled, and he looked over at his oldest daughter. She was the spitting image of her mother and so much like her brother that it was no wonder most everyone assumed Max was her father.

"What do you mean?"

"I want to stay here for the rest of summer."

"You loved St. Barts as a little girl," he said, going back to eating.

"She can stay with us," Max said finally, picking up his wine glass and looking at his dad. The challenge was on.

"That's not necessary, Maxton. We've already booked the trip. It would be a waste of money to cancel anything."

"Maxton" was the warning.

"She's sixteen, Dad. She deserves the right to decide how she spends her time, and she would be staying with family. No imposition or cost to you. If it's that big of a deal, I'll cover any costs you don't get back," Max told him before taking a bite of food.

"It's more than that," Carrie said, taking his father's hand in her own.

Max looked away. This was too weird and too much. He never should have agreed to this. Carrie was a fling, something to kill time in Africa, and now here she was with his father who had a tendency to date young and marry quickly. It happened with Brinkley's mom. And it was happening again.

"We wanted it to be a surprise," his father said.

"What kind of surprise?" Jules asked, laying a hand on Max's knee to reassure him, reminding him she was there, and he wasn't alone.

"We were planning to get married," he said, setting down his silverware and looking at his son, still holding Carrie's hand.

Max held his eye contact for a moment before looking at Carrie. It was a challenge. Would one of them say anything?

"So, it's a family affair," Max said sarcastically, looking away from her.

"To be fair, when we made the arrangements, I figured you and Jules were broken up, divorced if I'm correct. You had just come home, and I just assumed you would not be available to leave for an extended vacation so soon."

"A wedding takes a whole month to perform?" Max asked.

"Obviously not. How long was your ceremony? Five minutes?" his dad quipped back.

"I've suddenly lost my appetite," Max said, pushing back his chair and grabbing his glass of wine.

"Rani, can you watch the kids so we can all talk this out?" Jules asked softly before getting out of her own chair and following Max.

He was refilling his glass and staring out the window when she walked up.

"I underestimated the dinner."

"It's not your fault."

"I shouldn't have pushed you to come," Jules said. "Let's just get Baer and go home."

"I feel like I'm going to spend the rest of my life skating around half truths," Max told her as she wrapped her arms around him. He buried his nose in her hair and sighed. "Wanna make out until my dad finds us?"

"No," she said with a smile, pushing away from him. He took her hand and pulled her back in, their lips touching in a simple kiss. She felt his free hand start sliding down her hip and pulled it away, lacing her fingers with his. She knew what game he was playing.

"I love you," he whispered.

"I love you, too," she said back. "No touching," she whispered with a wink.

"Is the tantrum over?" his father asked, and Jules felt him immediately tense up.

"You may not approve of my marriage, you are free to make light of it when we're not around if it makes you feel better, but if we're comparing it to what you're doing right now, you have no right. Assault me all you want, but do not treat Jules that way. Especially after all she has done to keep this family together and your children safe."

"If you hadn't run off at the first chance to Africa, Jules wouldn't have been alone to take care of anything. It was business. I had to go. Jules graciously offered to help out," his father retorted.

"For a week or two maybe. Four months? Six months? Would you have left her there for a year?" Max growled.

"You did," his father shot back, the first time his temper came out in front of other people. Even if he was right, it felt like his own father punched him in his newly healed sternum.

"Maybe everyone should take a deep breath and sit down, and we can talk this out," Carrie suggested. This wasn't the John she knew, but it's a version Max had described one night in Africa. The same night they played their own version of drunken confessions and ended up having sex for the first time. Max had told her point blank he was still in love with someone else and being with her wouldn't change that. But they were both lonely in Africa, so what the hell?

"This doesn't involve you," Max told her. Jules laid a hand on his arm, anything to keep his anger in check.

"Actually, it does. I'm marrying your father," she said.

"I've known Jules a long time. What's your excuse? Why

can't you be happy for me? Why is there always a motive?" Max asked.

"Unfortunately, Max, there is a certain decorum required with our family. There are expectations and guidelines. You obviously bypassed them all with your desire to become a doctor. You cheated the system when you married Jules and produced an heir."

"How are you any different? Like father, like son? You've only known Carrie a few months."

"Max," Carrie said softly.

"I'm done with the secrets. This needs to be out in the open," Max told them.

"We don't keep secrets," Carrie told him, taking his father's hand. "He knows everything."

Max felt anger and sadness and a tornado of emotions well up inside him. "When?" he asked. She confessed her relationship with Max to his father, and they were still getting married. Was that why he was lashing out today? To prove he is the better man for Carrie?

"After that first time I saw you when we came back. I don't expect you to understand. Love is a funny thing. But I'm not here because of you, I'm not here for money. I'm here because I met your father, and it just felt right and easy. I love him."

"It's my fault we weren't going to include you on the trip for the wedding. I thought it would be awkward," she continued.

"I thought you had enough to deal with. The divorce, the injury, Jules, and the baby. I thought by staying away I was doing something right," his father said. "I wanted to give you space to put your life back in order. Figure out your priorities."

Jules took a deep breath, catching John's glance and

almost imperceptibly shook her head. Max ran a hand through his hair. He didn't even know what thought to land on. *What baby? He looked over at Jules, but for the life of him he couldn't tell what the look in her eyes meant.*

He looked back at his father. "I'm a grown adult, and it's about time you start treating me like one. Baer is six years old. Not a baby. I have to live with my decisions, but they are mine. Stop trying to control them or decide for me. And stop doing it to Rani."

"She's a child."

"She's almost seventeen. She graduates high school this year. She's halfway through college with all her extra credits. She's a straight-A student, she earns her own money, she's responsible, she's kind and compassionate. She has a free mind, and she deserves to be treated like she has a voice and choice," Max told him.

"Mom died. It sucked. Justine died. That sucked, too. But you disappeared, mentally and physically, and it's been Rani and I fending for ourselves. It's time to adjust your expectations and your priorities for the future of this family. Riches aren't everything."

"Says the kid who's had it all his whole life."

Max shook his head. "I didn't have it all in Africa. I slept on dirt cots, I didn't shower for days, sometimes food was scarce. I saw more death than I will in a lifetime, and I saved more lives in one day than I might in a year here. My money didn't get me anything there. Just knowledge."

"Can't buy happiness either," his father said. "Listen, if you guys want to come on the trip, or just for the wedding, you can come."

"Thanks for the pity invite, Dad. But you were right. I have work, and I don't think I'm ready to start calling Carrie, Mom." Max finished his glass and set it down on the coffee table. It was fine if his dad wanted to pretend everything was okay, but Max would need more time adjusting.

"We could make it a double wedding," his dad suggested. "If you and Jules are officially considering getting back together."

"Thanks, but no thanks. Let's go," Max said heading for the door.

"Maxton, I'm trying here," his father called after him. "You spend all this time blaming me for leaving my kids where I knew they would be safe and cared for, and you did the same thing. You left your son, and you left Jules. I was the one who was here for them. I was the one who helped Jules," he said.

"Until you left, too," Max pointed out.

"John, it's okay. We know," Jules said, cutting him off. It took Max a moment to look away from his father to her. Things started to click into place, comments, diversions, six months lost. Jules reassures his father, her sudden trip to visit him in Africa where they spent more time apart because of a last-minute emergency at the clinic, her silence and hesitancy for anything physical between them. When she left, Carrie was the one who showed up with kind words. He hated to think what secret Jules might be hiding from him after all this time.

"I have to go," Max said, brushing off Jules as she tried to stop him. He couldn't do this now. He was just starting to think that everything was going to be fine.

"Don't leave," his father said.

Max didn't even answer, and he didn't wait as he headed for the front door, letting it slam on his way out. It didn't take long for Rani and the kids to come running in.

"Where's Max?" she asked.

"He had to go," Jules told her with a soft smile. "Baer, let's pack up and go, too. It's almost past your bedtime."

"Jules," John said as she opened the front door to follow Max.

"Just leave it alone. This is between me and Max now."

"What did you do?" Rani yelled before running upstairs and slamming her bedroom door shut.

John sighed. "It's okay, Daddy. I still love you," Brinkley said, taking his hand. Carrie took his other hand and gave it a squeeze.

"Baby steps," she said.

"You don't know Max," he said.

"Actually, I do. I could tell you some stories of Africa," she said with a smile.

26

SAME NIGHT

He didn't know what to feel when he got home. He was pissed at his father for acting like this was nothing. He was angry at Carrie for cursing him out one day and jumping into bed with his dad the next. He hated himself for ever going to Africa, for running away when things were tough, for being just like his father. He was scared that because of him, Jules suffered, and she never told him.

The only thing he ever did right was medicine.

"Okay, baby. Run upstairs and get changed into your PJs and brush your teeth. I'll be up in a minute for stories," he heard Jules say as the front door closed.

He poured a glass of scotch and forced himself to take a slow sip, letting it coat his mouth before swallowing, feeling the burn. He was watching the entry, waiting for her to come through. She stopped just inside and looked at him.

"I can't do this," Max said. Not necessarily the right thing to say but at least Jules knew exactly what situation he was talking about.

"So, maybe we shouldn't have gone to your dad's for dinner," she tried to joke with a smile. He didn't smile back.

"I have screwed up every relationship in my life. I deserve to be alone. I used Meg, I used Carrie." He looked down into the glass. "I use you."

"That's not true," she said. She didn't move from her spot. She needed to let him process. Just like she processed almost a year ago.

"Really? I used you to get my family's money. I used you to get the bonus inheritance. I used you to take care of every-thing when I just left town. I used you to become a mom of three kids because I couldn't do it alone. I used you when I was lonely and horny and happy, and I took it all out on you when I was angry and upset."

"Max, you realize I've always had a choice. To stay or go. To put up with it or leave. To stand by you or to let you go. You are a good man, a good person, a good father, a good friend, and a good husband."

"I don't see a lot of good going on right now," he said.

"A rough patch."

"According to my father, I have a lot of those."

"I don't care about your father."

"You cared enough to let him take care of you," Max said, raising an eyebrow at her. "You cared enough about him to let him just leave and saddle you with three kids to take care of with no real idea when he would be back." He finished his drink. "You care."

"Max, just sit down so we can talk."

"I can't do that right now because I don't want to say anything that I will regret, and I can't handle it if you're going to tell me you're another notch on my father's bedpost."

He knew he already took it too far, but he couldn't get a handle on the emotions. Jules was the one thing he always counted on, and he was sabotaging it. All he wanted was to have her hold him and tell him it would all be okay, but the fear of failure and inadequacy inside him kept his guard up.

"I had a miscarriage," she told him. Max just looked at her. "Almost three months after you left. I woke up in the middle of the night bleeding, and your dad took me to the hospital."

Without realizing it, the glass in Max's hand shattered, sending glass in all directions. He hadn't even realized he was squeezing it so tight. How had he been so blind to what else she might have been going through?

"Shit, Max," Jules said before rushing to the wet bar for a towel and pressing it onto his hand. After a minute she lifted it, the blood already starting to pool again. "Keep the pressure. Let me go grab my kit."

"No," he said, using his other hand to grab her arm. "I love you. I'm sorry," he pulled her close and kissed her temple before he started for the door.

"Max, don't leave," she called.

"I just need to think," he said. "I just..." he trailed off looking back at her. He saw the tears in her eyes and quickly brushed away the few that cascaded down his cheek. He opened his mouth to speak, but nothing came to mind, so he turned, opened the front door, and walked out of the house.

It took everything in Jules' power to stay standing, to let him go and not beg him to stay, to realize he had to figure things out on his own and trust he would come back. She needed to be strong for their son. She needed to be strong for their family, she thought, as she laid a protective hand on her stomach.

HE WAS AN IDIOT. HOW MANY TIMES HAD HE REPEATED that to himself in the past ten years? How come when he was in the hospital, he was rational, confident, and in control, and yet the rest of his life kept feeling so out of control?

Max had no plan after he left the house, aside from silence, and hopefully a moment to gather his thoughts and feelings.

His father was marrying his ex-whatever. Jules miscarried their baby after he left. If the first was a shock, the second even more so. He left suddenly, but they still talked constantly. She came to see him. Why wouldn't she tell him? Would that have changed anything?

"I THOUGHT WE TALKED ABOUT THIS," JULES SAID.

"We did," Max told her, walking away from the papers on the table and opening his locker.

"We agreed to get divorced."

"We agreed to consciously uncouple," he pointed out.

"We still need divorce papers."

"Is there someone else?" he asked, afraid to turn around and see her face.

"No," she told him. "But it's not helping either one of us."

"Get laid by other people?" he asked, looking at her as he slammed his locker shut.

"Why are you mad?"

"I guess I just wasn't expecting divorce papers today. At work."

"Well, you moved out of the cottage. Our schedules aren't exactly in sync. I just thought this would be easier."

"To bring me divorce papers the morning after we have mind-blowing sex." He shrugged as he poured coffee. "Makes sense."

"*Max, how many times did we go over this? How many conversations? I thought this was what we agreed on.*" He didn't say anything. "*Are you changing your mind? Do you want to stay married?*" she asked.

Before he could respond, the door swung open.

"*Incoming two minutes out,*" Alex said. "*All hands on deck.*"

"*Max,*" Jules whispered as he downed his coffee.

"*It's fine,*" he said, taking a pen out of his pocket and looking down at the papers. He signed quickly, flipped a page, signed, and finally clicked his pen shut and put it back into his pocket. "*There. It's over.*"

He walked out of the room just in time to meet the incoming trauma.

"*Has anyone seen Max?*" Jules asked an hour later as she sent the last trauma to surgery.

"*Lounge,*" Alex told her just as Max came out with his bag.

"*Hey,*" she said. "*Do you have a second?*"

"*Not really.*" He walked outside, and she followed.

"*I want to talk about this. If it's not something you want, then maybe it's worth talking about.*"

"*You were the one who brought it up to begin with,*" he told her. "*Are you telling me you don't want it?*"

"*I'm saying maybe I was wrong to rush into it. You're my best friend, you're the father of my child. I don't want to lose you because I pushed us into something.*"

"*I pushed us into it to begin with, so I'll take the beginning and you can take the end, and we'll call it even,*" he told her.

"*Max, I just want to talk about it.*"

"*There's nothing more to talk about, but if I don't leave now, I'm going to be late.*"

"*Where are you going?*"

"I just need a break, so I took some time off."

"I thought you cancelled that." He shrugged. "When will you be back?" she asked.

"I don't know."

"Where are you going?" He hesitated. Asshole moment. "Max, where are you going?"

"Africa. My flight is in two hours."

"What about us?" she asked.

"A little time apart won't hurt us. Maybe that's what we both need," he told her before disappearing toward the parking lot.

Thinking back on the moment he walked away from her, he wondered if she already knew she was pregnant, or did that come later?

Max found an old shirt in his car and replaced the nearly soaked rag on his hand before getting out of the Range Rover and heading into the hospital. When in doubt, go to the hospital. He felt safe there.

He walked through the ambulance bay to the admit desk. At least it was quiet.

"Didn't your shift end a couple hours ago?" Bobby asked.

"Is Marco around?"

"Surgery."

"Meg?" he asked.

"Lounge."

Max nodded then headed down the hall. He pushed open the door with his good hand and found Meg and Kelley pouring coffee.

"Vampire hours again?" Meg asked.

"No. Got a second?" he asked with a quick glance at Kelley.

"Yeah. What's up?" he nodded as he headed out the door, letting it close behind himself. She was hot on his heels, a glance at his wrapped hand.

"Suture room," Max told her.

"What is going on?" she asked.

"I just need some help. I'll probably need the Max special, too," he said.

"Did you drive here?"

"I've had enough judgement for one day," he told her, pushing open the door.

"Want to tell me what happened?" she asked as he sat down on the bed, and she pulled over a tray.

"I broke a glass." She slowly pulled back the cloth, and his hand started bleeding.

"This is pretty deep." She replaced the shirt with gauze and disappeared out the door. Max laid back on the bed and closed his eyes. Maybe he could pretend to be somewhere else, back to a time when things were really good.

"Alright, do you care to tell me what happened?" Meg asked, walking back into the room and hanging the banana bag on the stand next to him. He held out his arm like a child and let her roll up the sleeve and easily insert the IV.

"I told you. I broke a glass."

"How?"

"I got a little upset, and I squeezed it too hard. I think."

Meg pulled up a stool next to him and slowly started removing the gauze before irrigating the wound to see what kind of damage was done.

"It could have been worse, but it's not great. One cut between your thumb and forefinger will need some stitches. Might as well put a couple in on the other side, too."

"Just numb up my hand and go for it."

"Why did you get upset?" she asked.

"This isn't a therapy session."

"I'm asking as a friend. No unsolicited advice."

"We had dinner with my father tonight. Things have been a little tense. He announced he was getting married next month."

"Wow. That seems kind of sudden, right? Justine died only a couple years ago."

"Yeah, and he's only been with Carrie for a few months."

"Is he happy?"

"I have no idea. All I keep thinking is that this is his pattern. Finds a younger girl, dates her, marries her quickly, then something happens. Brinkley and Rani have been through so much. They have each lost their moms, and these women come in, and they get attached."

"What if she's the one that lasts?"

He winced as she injected his hand to numb the areas.

"I don't know. Maybe she will."

"What's she like?" He shrugged as best he could lying down. "Come on. Dr. Meg is here to listen to all your woes."

"Very funny."

"Why aren't you letting Jules play nurse?"

"We kind of got in a fight. Or rather, I was an asshole, and I left."

"Sounds up to par," she joked. "You can't keep doing this to her."

"What?"

"Run hot and cold. Run away when there's a problem. If you want to be with her, you need to be with her."

"What if I'm not meant to be with anyone?"

"I know that's not true. If I had to bet everything I own, I would bet on you and Jules. The least you can do is stick it out with the woman you dumped me for."

"I didn't dump you for Jules. Jules just happened."

"Nothing just happens to you, Hudson."

"My life is a comedy of errors. I'm just waiting for the punchline or the finale."

"You're not the only one who has family drama, or relationship strains, or work issues. You come into this hospital, and everyone turns to you for guidance. You lead day in and day out. You never hesitate. But the second you leave these doors, you lose all confidence."

He felt the skin in his hand pull and looked over to see her starting the first of the stitches.

"I thought you weren't giving advice."

"Too late."

"Everything will be fine with Jules. I'm not worried about that."

"What are you worried about?"

"The only thing I am good at is being a doctor. I'm just fumbling around aimlessly with the rest of it, hoping I don't accidentally drop my kid on his head, or kill a patient, or forget to buy milk at the store."

"All people go through that. It just comes with the territory of being an adult and a parent. You know all this stuff, you also chose to go to Africa where there was a different set of rules."

"I never should have gone to Africa."

"I disagree. I think you came back with a new vision. Your approach to medicine is different. Your patient care is more quality. Even your leadership has evolved. I know it might be hard for you to see the difference with everything that has been going on, but you're not failing at anything. If anything, the only thing you need to work on is your communication with Jules."

"Thanks, Dr. Phil."

"So, what did we learn in today's session?" Meg joked as the door opened, and Bobby poked his head in.

"We have an incoming five minutes out. Three to five victims double MVA. And Jules is on the phone."

"Tell her I'll call her back in a minute," Max said sitting up, one leg on either side of the gurney as Meg finished the stitches.

"Are you actually going to call her back?" Meg asked when Bobby left.

"Yes. I will call her back. I'm not avoiding her. I'm gathering my thoughts."

"Thoughts on what? Why are you and Jules even fighting about your dad getting married?"

"We aren't. It's something different."

"Something you don't want to talk about."

"Exactly." She stretched a bandaid over each cut then began wrapping gauze around his hand and wrist to keep it secure. "Good as gold. You know the drill."

"Thanks, Doc," he said before hopping off the gurney. He grabbed the banana bag with his bad hand, and Meg rolled her eyes as he squeezed it to get the fluids into his veins faster.

She headed to admit to wait for the incoming traumas, and Max found himself in the supply closet on the hunt for an ace bandage, before heading in her same direction.

"Hey, you," he said, motioning to an intern standing around and waiting for something to do. "Hold this bag up and keep squeezing it," he said, handing him the banana bag. The kid looked at Bobby and Meg who immediately turned and looked away.

Max picked up the phone and dialed Jules' number by heart.

"Hey," he said, cradling the phone against his ear as he

started to wrap his own hand and wrist with the bandage to protect it further.

"What are you doing?" Meg asked.

"Nothing," he replied before turning his attention back to the phone.

"I think I left my cell in the den," he told Jules. "I know. I'm sorry." He pinned the bandage and took the banana bag back from the intern just as the first patient started rolling in. He heard vitals and updates in the background.

"Max," Meg yelled as she headed down the hall. "We're going to need some help."

"Jules, I have to go. They have a big trauma coming in. I'll probably just sleep here." He sighed and rubbed his eyes, the sadness in her voice struck straight to the heart. "I love you. Nothing has changed. I just need some time to adjust."

Adjust how, she asked. "I have a lot of guilt. I went to Africa and abandoned you and Baer. If I stayed home, maybe things would be different. Maybe..." he trailed off as the next trauma rolled in, and Bobby went after it.

"Please, I need to do this my way. I can't let you take care of me and our family. I need to be able to take care of you." He could tell she was crying. "Jules, baby, please. I promise. Nothing is different with us. I need to go." He sighed and smiled softly. "I love you. I know I don't say it enough. I love you, Jules. Nothing is going to change that." The doors swung open. "Babe, I gotta go, for reals. Bring my phone."

He didn't wait for her to answer before he hung up. Without thinking, he pulled the IV out and grabbed the nearest piece of tissue to press into the crook of his elbow, raising his arm to hold it in place.

"What do we have?" he asked as he followed them down the hall.

27

SAME NIGHT

Meg tore off her gloves as she walked back to admit and tossed them in the nearest hazardous waste bin. A loss on a night shift sucked. Especially a kid. She just prayed everything they did worked.

She had to nearly force Max away from the body on the gurney. Over an hour trying to resuscitate after opening his chest, losing almost all the blood volume, and after Max threw a tray of instruments across the room refusing to give up, he started manual heart compressions and they started to see the vitals improve. It helped that he had his hand wrapped around a tear in the aorta.

"How's the kid?" Bobby asked when she walked up.

"Fingers crossed. Max is literally holding his heart in his hand to stop the bleeding."

"Should we be letting Max work on patients?" he asked with an eyebrow raise. "Banana bag?"

"He's fine. Just dehydrated and blood loss."

"Temper tantrum."

"Leave him alone," Meg said before disappearing into the

lounge for a cup of coffee. When she came back out, Bobby was talking all hands and smiles with a red head at the desk.

"Meg, where's Hudson?" Bobby called as she grabbed her charts to disappear into a dark corner to decompress.

"I told you thirty seconds ago. On his way up to surgery with that kid. Why?"

"He has a guest."

Meg looked at her watch. It was pushing 11 p.m. "Now? He's not even on shift."

"I know, I'm sorry. I thought he would probably be here," the woman said. "It sounds like he is."

"Who are you?" Meg asked. Max didn't need any more drama or shockers for one night, so if she could stop this and get the crazy out of the ER as a friend to Max, she would.

"This is Carrie," Bobby said. "Max's...dad's fiancé. So, Max's stepmom?" He grinned. *Max's stepmom was hot and young.*

"Hi, I'm Carrie," she reiterated. "I'm actually an old friend of Max's."

"You're John's girlfriend?" Meg asked.

"Fiancé," Carrie said hesitantly, slowly letting her hand drop when Meg didn't take it. "You know John?"

This took tonight and Max's issues to a whole new level. An old friend of Max's. John's fiancé. Young fiancé.

"Max is busy," Meg told her.

"I'm happy to wait."

"It's a free country," Meg said. Now she couldn't hide, she needed to be out in the open and hopefully stop a train wreck.

She didn't have to wait long before she saw his tall, tan, and toned figure pass down a side hall. He went in one door of an exam room, opened some drawers, and finally came out the other side. His trauma gown was gone, but there were still traces of blood on his shirt and pants from him diving in before he was fully covered.

"Son of a bitch," Max said, walking up to admit. "Can you help me out?" he asked Meg, tossing her a new ace bandage roll.

"Not with this," she told him, throwing it back. She held up a roll of black CoFlex tape. "What did you do?"

The top half of the previous ace bandage along his forearm was covered in blood. He was wearing only one glove, which he was already using to remove the bandage from his arm.

"Max," a voice called, and he looked over to the chairs to see Carrie.

"I don't have time for you right now," he said before swiftly walking through the double doors and into the lounge, Meg hot on his heels.

"This night got a little more interesting," Meg told him as he flopped onto the couch and finished unwrapping his arm. He sighed when he found that the blood from the patient hadn't soaked into his own gauze bandage. But it didn't stop his newly sutured hand from oozing blood.

Meg pulled up a chair and fully unwrapped his hand and looked at the stitches.

"You didn't pop any."

"I could have told you that."

"So, who's Carrie?" she asked as she started doctoring him back up.

"That would be my dad's fiancé."

"She's young."

"Yes, she is." He laid his head back and closed his eyes.

"She also said she's an old friend of yours."

One eye popped open and looked at her before closing again.

"Explains a lot."

"Explains nothing."

"Explains why you're having a hard time with your dad marrying her. If you're old friends, that's like your dad marrying your high school sweetheart."

"Carrie is not my high school sweetheart."

"You know what I mean. There," she said, securing the bandage. "Please just keep it low key if you're sticking around."

"I'll probably crash in the suture room."

"Not going home to Jules?"

"Not tonight, nosy," he said before standing up and opening his locker, relieved to find a set of scrubs. "Go guard the door so I can change really fast," he said.

She did as he asked, and a few minutes later, he walked out freshly clean with a cup of coffee.

"Who is she?" Meg asked.

"I met her in Africa," he said with a shrug.

"You met Carrie in Africa?" He didn't say anything. "You had an affair with Carrie in Africa." Max just looked at her and took a sip of his coffee. "Oh, that makes a lot of sense now."

"Karma is a bitch," he said, walking up to the desk and looking at the board. "I think my job is done here."

"Max," Carrie said, standing up and walking over.

"I'm not going to say it again," he told her, knowing full well everyone was watching them.

"I don't care. All I need is fifteen minutes."

"To what? Change my mind? Try and convince me that my father is not the person I think he is?"

"Max, just go take care of it," Meg whispered to him before using her shoulder to push him toward the ambulance bay doors.

"Fine," he said. He stalked out, and Carrie followed.

"What did you do to your hand?" she asked.

"You wanted to talk about my dad, talk about my dad. That's it."

"I'm not making excuses for him. I'm just telling you what I know. You intimidate him." Max laughed. "Hear me out. In his eyes, you defied everything he was setting up for you — to become a doctor. A very successful doctor. You never let wealth and privilege hold you back. He told me your story, as he knows it, sitting on the sidelines. And I saw the pride and love he has for you and who you have become."

"He has a funny way of showing it."

"You don't need him. But he needs you. And he's too afraid and probably too proud to tell you." She watched his head drop and the fingers on his good hand run through his hair. "I know about your mom. I know about Justine. Just like I think you are right now, he's trying to find his way back. In order to do that, he had to leave. Which meant he had to leave everything to you."

"Why are you telling me this? Why isn't he down here telling this to me?"

"Because he doesn't think you'll talk to him. He knows he screwed up mentioning the baby." Max just looked at her. Did she know everything about him now? In Africa, they were casual acquaintances who only had death and famine in common. Now their lives intersected.

"This isn't something that is going to turn into a happy little family overnight."

"I know."

"I might be with Jules, but it's awkward as fuck knowing a woman I had a relationship with is sleeping with my father."

"I know."

"My whole life, he's only pointed out where I've messed up or how I didn't do what he wanted. He has never once acknowledged that he was happy for me, or proud of what I had become, or God forbid he admits that my Grami left everything to me and not to him."

"What do you think it feels like to be the person who ran the household for decades, the one who managed the money and took care of everyone, the man who had three children with no mothers to support, and suddenly he's not the caretaker anymore."

"I appreciate what you are doing, but you coming here in the middle of the night isn't going to magically fix things."

"I don't want to fix things. I don't think you're broken. I think there's a communication breakdown."

"What is it with today? Everyone wants to play shrink." He tossed his empty cup into the trash can and turned toward the door.

"Max, please don't shut him out."

"I'm not shutting him out. I'm focusing on my life and what I can control. Stop forcing the Brady Bunch and just let things be and happen how they happen."

"I have a feeling if I just let things happen, you would be the stranger next door."

"What do you want? To be best friends? Sunday dinners, picnics in the park, family reunions, waking up together on Christmas morning and carving a turkey for Thanksgiving? I'm barely keeping my shit together as it is, Carrie. I'm not much of a planner, I don't think into the future, I'm living moment by moment. If you want the warm and fuzzies, then talk to Jules. If you're bleeding, I'll fix you. I can't fix emotions."

"Fine. I give up. I guess it was too much to ask that you finally try to have a good relationship with your father."

"It's a little hard to start down that road when he's sleeping with my ex... whatever," he yelled, turning to face her. He took a deep breath and turned away with a deep sigh, dragging his hands through his hair in typical Max fashion, before rubbing his face.

He turned back. "I'm sorry," he said. "I'm an asshole. It's basically tattooed on my forehead. I appreciate you coming down here in the middle of the night to try to talk to me, but you can't solve this overnight. This is years of issues. I need to focus on my immediate family, Jules and Baer. I need to mend what I broke by running away. Until I can get that guilt under control and forgive myself, there's no room for forgiving anyone else."

"Sounds like you're shrinking yourself," she told him with a smirk.

"I've had a lot of practice lately."

"I'm sorry that I pushed this. I guess I never realized how deep it went. Especially when the only side I know is John's."

"I hope you don't take this the wrong way, but that's probably the only side you will know. And every story has two sides. I'm not an open book, and if I do turn a page, I need to do it for Jules."

"You really love her."

"I don't think I knew what love was until Jules. I hurt a lot of people along the way, you included. I hurt Jules even more, I'm sure."

"I knew what I was getting myself into with you. There was a void, and I filled it. I can't be upset about it now, not if I plan to marry your father."

He grimaced.

"Get used to it, because as much as you think this is a passing trend with him, I'm not planning on going anywhere."

Max kept his mouth shut instead of spouting the first sarcastic remark. "Just give it time," he said after a while.

"Okay," she said.

"And maybe I can start with asking for a favor." She just looked at him. "Have Baer over for a sleepover tomorrow..." he trailed off, looking at his watch.

"Well, technically tonight."

"We'd like that."

"I think Jules and I could use some time to work out a few kinks."

"Oh, yeah," she said with a smile.

"Not those kinks."

"No problem. We'd be happy to have him. I know Brinkley is kind of struggling with them being apart. It's my understanding they shared a room when they were with you."

"Yeah. Basically twins."

"It's sweet."

"Just have Rachel pack up anything Baer needs or wants. She knows the drill. Rani knows it all, too."

"You're staying?" she asked.

"Easier to stay and sleep a few hours. Which I am going to do right now. If another trauma comes in, I'm doomed."

"Have a good night, Max."

He waved it off and turned to walk inside to have all eyes turn to him. Marco had suddenly made an appearance and turned to cross his arms in reprimand.

"What?" Max asked.

"Who was that?" Marco asked.

"Carrie," he said casually.

"Carrie," Marco repeated.

"Yeah."

"Carrie."

"Pretty sure I already said that."

"Carrie Carrie?"

"Who is Carrie Carrie?" Bobby asked with a smile.

"I'm going to bed. Wake me up at seven," he said before heading down the hall. Marco didn't wait for him to get far before following.

"Need a surgeon to look at those sutures to make sure Dr. Meg did a good job?" Marco grinned.

"They're fine. Give it a couple of days."

"You shouldn't be using that hand."

"I'll live."

"What is Carrie doing here?"

"Trying to solve world peace between me and my father."

"Max, buddy, sometimes I'm really glad I don't have your life."

"Marco, me, too. Now leave me alone," he said, opening the door to sutures. He prayed he would sleep for at least five hours. It only took about one to finally fall asleep.

28

THE NEXT MORNING

His hand was killing him. That's what woke him up. Not the voices outside the door, the banging of trauma beds, drunks singing Christmas carols. He was used to sleeping through nearly everything.

The sound of his name, a child crying, the touch of a woman, gunshots, pain. He couldn't sleep through any of that.

For a moment, he even forgot where he was as he fumbled for his phone and couldn't find the nightstand. His injured hand collided with a suture table and sent metal clattering to the floor.

"Fuck," he whispered into the dark, running a hand over his eyes. Now the throbbing was worse. The door opened, and a stream of violent light from the fall fell into his eyes.

"Good, you're awake," Meg said.

"What time is it?" he asked, closing his eyes.

"Almost six."

"I'm not on yet."

"Early morning house fire. Two adults. Two kids. And a

B&E, boyfriend is critical, girlfriend was raped."

"I'm coming," he said, swinging his feet to the ground. She held the door open for him.

"You have time for a quick cup of coffee and do something with your hair."

"What's wrong with my hair?" She just looked at him as they walked into the lounge. Max opened his locker. He swung his stethoscope around his neck and fumbled with the only hair tie he could find, hot pink, and secured his unruly hair into a manbun.

"Here," Meg said, handing him a cup of coffee which he proceeded to chug, his mouth only burning a little. He stuck in a piece of gum and closed his locker.

"It's scary how you can just turn it on like that," she said. He poured another cup of coffee.

"What?" he asked as they walked out of the room. "Hey Alex, can you find me some ibuprofen?" he yelled once they got close to the desk.

"Mad Max turns into Dr. Cool turns into Man Bun."

"I don't know what you're talking about," he said with a smirk.

"Got a rager of a hangover?" Alex asked.

"No, I have ten stitches in my hand, and I'm still not afraid to beat you," he said with a smile and soothing voice, like the one he would use when he was trying to get Brinkley and Baer to go to sleep. Alex almost believed he was saying something nice.

"Mad Max."

He finished the second cup of coffee, tossed it into the trash, and grabbed gloves. "Who else is on?"

"Marco is coming from downstairs. Bobby is here. I think Dani is on at seven. We paged her, so hopefully sooner. Jules at eight, I think. Interns."

"So, it's me and you?"

"Dr. Cool," she said with a smile.

"How bad are the fire victims?"

"Minor burns and smoke inhalation mainly."

"Quick assessment. Can the interns handle them?"

She shrugged. "No time like the present." The flashing lights lit up the darkness, and they rushed outside to meet the two ambulances.

"What do we have?" Max asked.

"Father and son. Smoke inhalation, trapped upstairs before rescue could get them out. No burns on the kid, but dad has some on his hands from the door and from protecting his kid."

"Kid to Curtain 1; Dad to Trauma 2. Curtis, follow them both," Max said, yelling to an intern.

"Mom and the second boy made it downstairs but got trapped when the stairs collapsed," the second paramedic said.

"Meg, take them to Curtains 2 and 3. I want to leave Trauma 1 open for the B&E."

Max didn't have to wait long for two more ambulances to roll up.

"Nothing like starting the party early," the paramedic said as he opened the back door. "Boyfriend, unconscious, lots of bruising, head wound. Hasn't woken up yet. Pressure's pretty low, but he responds to pain."

"Take him to Trauma 2," Max said. "I'm right behind you."

"This is Maggie. Cuts and contusions, possible concussion, and she was raped."

"Did someone call for a doctor," Dani said running up.

"Perfect timing. Take the girlfriend. Exam 3," Max said

without hesitation before turning to run and follow the boyfriend.

Dani tossed her stuff at Alex at the desk and escorted the gurney to Exam 3.

"How are you doing in here?" Meg asked, pushing through the door to Trauma 1 to find Max and Marco up to their elbows in blood.

"About ready to take him up to surgery," Marco said.

"Lots of internal bleeding. This guy must have taken a metal bat to the stomach," Max said. "I think he's stable enough for a quick CT. I'm worried about the head, too."

"If he can keep his pressure up," Marco said, landing one last stitch to the hole in the heart that Max was plugging with his finger. "Okay, you can move your hand now."

Max stepped back, bloody gloves in the air. "It's holding."

"Okay, let's go. I'll keep you posted," Marco said before helping push the gurney out.

"How's the family?"

"Dad has some pretty good burns but should heal with minimal scarring. Mom got a little bit, too, on her arm and neck, trying to shield the youngest son before rescue could get to them. Kids just have smoke inhalation."

"Good," Max said, peeling off his gloves and gown. "I could use a shower," he said, pulling at his damp scrub top.

"And a new bandage." She looked at his hand. He went to make a fist and winced.

"Yeah, I might have pulled a couple stitches."

"Of course you did."

"How is Dani doing with the girlfriend?"

"She is pretty withdrawn. Social worker is coming down."

"Did they catch the guy?"

"Not yet."

"Damn."

Max glanced at his watch. "I have thirty minutes until my shift starts."

"I got us covered. Go shower," she said.

He didn't have to be asked twice. The shower was the perfect remedy for the past twelve hours. It washed away his residual anger, it smoothed the edges of uncertainty, it created a clear head to see Jules, and he also smelled better.

He was toweling off his hair in only scrub pants and sneakers when he heard someone clear their throat. He looked up and smiled at Jules holding two cups of coffee and a paper bag.

"Hi," he said.

"Hi." She walked over to the bench in front of him and sat down, setting out both cups of coffee and the bag. "I brought you breakfast."

"Thank you." He straddled the bench next to her then leaned over their breakfast, wrapping a hand around her neck and pulled her in for a lingering kiss.

"Late night?" she asked softly when he finally pulled away.

"I got a few hours of sleep."

"How's your hand?" he looked at the gauze that was oozing slightly. He still needed a couple of new stitches.

"We can fix it up after rounds. Meg might kill us if we're late." After a minute, he stood up and grabbed the new scrub top and slipped it on before affixing all his credentials, phone, and pager, then grabbed his cup of coffee and half a bagel to eat on the way.

He led the way to the door but stopped just before opening it, turned back to her, and kissed her again. "Sorry, I just can't help myself," he whispered against her lips.

She took the opportunity and, with coffee and food in

hand, stood on her tiptoes and wrapped her arms around his neck, breathing in his fresh shower scent.

"Never be sorry," she told him before kissing his neck.

He finally pulled back and opened the door letting her leave first. They were coming down the last flight of stairs to the ER when he broke the silence.

"So, I made arrangements for Baer to stay the night at my dad's," he said casually.

She looked over at him, slowing her pace. "Really? What's with the change of heart?"

"Long story, that I promise to tell you later, but Carrie showed up here last night, and I asked if they would mind having him over so you and I could have some time alone."

"That's a big change of heart from twelve hours ago."

"I know. I guess I have to start somewhere. Besides, when was the last time just the two of us had a whole night alone?" he asked, with a smile that bordered on wicked versus sweet.

"Never seemed to have a problem finding time before," she joked back.

"Okay, being serious. I think we deserve it, and I owe you."

"Owe me for what?"

"Putting up with me." He shrugged casually as they reached admit where everyone was gathering. He stuffed the rest of the bagel into his mouth as they found empty spots.

Maine gave them a quick glance before looking at the board.

"Smoke inhalation in Curtains 1 through 3," she said.

"I'll keep them," Max said, taking the four charts from her.

"And the rape in Exam 3?"

"Mine," Dani said, holding up the chart.

"Busy night. One in surgery, right?" Maine asked.

"The boyfriend. I haven't heard from Marco how he's doing," Max informed them.

"What else is rollover?" she asked.

"World's worst migraine in two, and drunk sleeping it off in one," Meg said.

"That's a nice way to start the morning. Jules, take the migraine and the drunk. Meg and Bobby, go take a nap," she said.

Meg handed off the two charts to Jules with a salute, and the group disbanded before Maine could throw anything else their way.

"Hudson," she called before he could get five steps away.

"I'll meet you in sutures," Jules whispered before quickly disappearing, so she wasn't held back.

"Yes ma'am," he said, turning toward Maine.

"I heard there was an incident," she said.

"I don't know what you're talking about?" She pointed to his hand. "Just a flesh wound. Nothing to worry about."

"We need those hands to fix people."

"I did alright last night during trauma. I'm okay."

"You're bleeding."

"I popped a stitch. I promise, we're good."

"Did you also attend said trauma under the influence?" she asked.

"No."

"I know when you're lying, Max."

"I'm not lying. I had a couple drinks at dinner, and I cut my hand. I needed to hydrate to help with the blood loss. Ask Meg."

"You better pray that nothing in those traumas comes back as a mistake."

"I didn't make any mistakes," he told her.

"I hope not. Clean up that hand. Take it easy for the day.

Lead trauma but no heavy procedures."

"Okay."

"I'm still waiting for your application for chief," she told him before he could walk off.

"I'm still thinking about it," he told her. He didn't wait for her to continue the conversation before walking off.

"What'd she want?" Jules asked when he finally joined her in sutures and sat down across from her.

"Asked about my hand, and verified I wasn't drunk when I opened up a victim's chest a few hours ago. And wanted to know why I hadn't turned in my application for chief."

Her hands stilled a beat before she turned her focus back on his hand and the small areas that needed new stitches.

"I told her already that you were a better candidate, and I wasn't planning on applying."

"Why not?" she asked. "You would be great. Everyone looks up to you."

"I am not a paper person, I'm not into politics, and if I wanted to be in charge, I would be running my family's company instead of medicine."

"Maybe we can be a joint task force."

"My vote is on you, and I promise to side with you on every issue."

"What if my issue is with you?"

"That's already a given," he said with a smile. She wrapped his hand in gauze then again with CoFlex tape.

"Now be a good boy and keep your bandage and hand dry for a couple days."

"Do I get a lollipop?" he asked.

"Maybe later." She stripped off her gloves and tossed them into the nearest trash can. "Now get to work."

"Hey, I thought I was in charge today."

"Not when Maine is around."

29

THAT NIGHT

Max tilted his head back to rest on the coffee table, letting his eyes close with a sigh. He felt the exhaustion from the top of his head to his toes. He managed to grab another quick shower at the hospital after a nearly severed arm and artery sprayed him in blood.

It must have been another full moon because each trauma was replaced with a new one. They ran out of beds, the hall was packed with minor injuries, and they had to start a second patient board. Jules agreed to stay an extra hour to discharge as many patients as possible.

Now she was upstairs taking her own shower. He knew he was exhausted when he couldn't even muster the strength to try and join her. Tonight wasn't supposed to be about romance and sex. It was for them to talk things through.

A night for him to man up.

He raised the glass to his lips and took a sip.

"Déjà vu," Jules whispered, seeing him sitting in the den looking like the walking dead, nursing a drink, much like the day he came home from Africa.

He opened an eye to look at her.

"No fair, you look way more comfortable and refreshed," he said, sitting up farther to take in her cut-off shorts and one of his well-worn Boise State football t-shirts.

"Need anything?" she asked, walking over to the wet bar. He shook his head.

She grabbed a bottle of water, and instead of taking up residence in the arm chair across from him, she slid down next to him, her legs under the coffee table opposite of his, hip to hip facing him.

"You could have showered again. Or changed."

"Too much effort," he said with a smile. He laid a hand on her thigh and squeezed.

"I'm sorry I didn't tell you," Jules finally said, breaking the ice. She was leaning back on both hands just watching him, t-shirt stretched tight against her chest. Of course Max noticed when he opened his eyes again.

"When did you find out?" he asked.

"A couple weeks after you left. My cycle was already late, but I'd been so stressed out, working long hours. I didn't really think about it until after you were gone."

"I never should have left."

"Max, we can't keep thinking about the past. We can't go back and change anything. I have no regrets. About you or my life. I don't want you to, either. What happened, happened."

"I should have been with you, not my dad. I should have been there for you."

"Stop 'shoulding' yourself. We all make choices, and most of the time, we think they are right at the moment. All we can do is learn from them."

He took a sip and looked over at her. She looked like a

sunset, her blonde hair starting to wave as it dried, her cheeks flushed, her blue eyes vibrant.

"I learned I never want to leave you again. I'm sorry it took me going all the way to Africa, a divorce, everything, to realize it."

"If I could have done one thing differently, I wouldn't have pushed so hard to separate and divorce."

"Why did you?"

"I think at the time, I thought it was too good to be true. I fell in love with you, and it scared me, and it wasn't planned. We never once talked about a real future. We just lived every day. I thought maybe I was holding the famous Maxton Hudson back from his soulmate."

"You're my soulmate. I wish I hadn't been so scared back then to tell you the moment I realized it."

"When did you realize it?" she asked with a smile.

"Remember that big fight I had with Meg in the trauma?"

"When you broke up?"

He nodded and took a sip. He needed some liquid courage. "That night you brought me along on your date in case things got weird. I rescued you from that creep trying to feel you up on the dance floor."

"I remember that creep."

"I walked over to you, put my hand around your waist, and practically dragged you away from him. He tried to fight me, and I accidentally elbowed him in the eye." He grinned a little. "You called me your hero, but you'd had quite a few drinks, so I don't even think you knew what you were doing. I let you drag me to the dance floor."

"Max," she said softly. She remembered it all.

"I took one look at you with your hair perfectly curled, bright red lipstick, this short royal blue lace dress and knee-high boots. You brushed your hair back, this guy tugged on a strand of your hair, you fake laughed before tugging on your earlobe. I was so jealous of him. But then, after we got rid of him, when you whispered in my ear, your hands grabbing on to my shirt to pull me closer, the first thing that popped into my mind was, 'I wish I was good enough to be with Jules.'"

He finished the bronze liquid in his glass and set it behind his head on the coffee table before looking at her.

Her blue eyes were glistening, but she wasn't smiling. Did he go too far? If so, he might as well go for broke.

"That's when it started for me. You asked me when I came back, why I thought that was the beginning of us. That was the night that I looked at you and the rest of the world blurred away. I took you to my house and put you to bed, and we never talked about it again. I went to work every day trying to play it cool, to keep being your best friend. When all I wanted was to know what it would feel like to kiss you. So, I agreed to the stupid auction, and I begged you to go with me, the whole time knowing that if I didn't take my chance then, I might not ever get it."

He watched her as a tear rolled down her cheek. She didn't move to wipe it away. He slowly reached for her, pulling her to kneel over his thighs. He brushed three tears away with his thumb before sitting up a little to kiss her cheek where the rest remained.

"I didn't know what to do with my feelings. Things I have never felt before. The more I wanted you, the more scared I got, and the more I started screwing up. I thought it was too good to be true. How did I get so lucky to have you?"

"Max," she whispered.

"I promise, I will do everything in my power to be the man you deserve, and the father Baer can look up to. I will repair my relationship with my dad. I will be friends with Carrie. Whatever I have to do. Whatever you need me to do."

She kissed him. She took it from his playbook, the only way to get him to stop talking was to kiss him. Her fingers gripped his hair as she arched into him, deepening their kiss.

"Maxton," she whispered. This was serious.

"Jules," he whispered back, his fingers digging into her hip, trailing down her back, cupping her cheek, tangling in her hair before pulling slightly to expose her neck. He kissed her jaw, her pulse, the curve of her shoulder.

With a free finger he pulled out the top of her t-shirt, and like a teenager, snuck a peek to see what she was wearing under it.

Nothing.

He groaned.

"Maxton," she said a little louder, and he let go of the shirt to look at her. "I need you to do something for me."

"Anything," he said with a grin.

"Not that. Yet." She smiled at him.

"Okay," he said softly, realizing they were still in serious business talk.

"I want you to apply for Chief of Emergency Medicine."

"I already told you, I think you're better suited for the job."

"And you bring new insight and experience from your time in Africa. You always talked about using your money for good. You could start an exchange program. Send our doctors to help in Africa. Help bring patients to the U.S. for cases we can help solve. Create new programs. Save lives. The stuff you hate, you'll figure it out. Maybe they would let me be your second in command."

"Why? You have these ideas. Why don't you do it, and I'll be your second. I'll give you all the money you want."

She held his gaze, he watched her lick her lips, her hands

clutching his shirt. A fresh tear cascaded down her cheek, and he was paralyzed with fear.

"Are you sick?" he asked quietly. Is this what his dad went through with Justine? His heart started beating so fast, he was sure Jules could see it through his shirt.

"No," she said before looking up at him with a smile. "I'm pregnant."

The End

ACKNOWLEDGMENTS

Writing the acknowledgments seems to be harder than writing the actual story because there are many people to thank, going all the way back to grade school, when I wrote my first story in 4th grade and decided that I wanted to be a writer when I grew up. It took this many years to finally take the leap and publish my first novel.

I owe the most thanks to my parents who let me spend years hiding out in my room writing (instead of playing outside), hogging our first desktop computer writing fanfiction, spending endless paychecks on spiral bound notebooks and pens, and always encouraging me to just keep writing.

Thank you to my tribe of family and friends who gave feedback, let me rant and whine and complain, were my first readers, and helped make the tough decision of a cover design.

To Heidy for helping me write my own bio because writing about ourselves is tough.

To Jan for being the first to see the cover and share in the excitement as each piece of this book fell into place over the summer.

To Anna & Words with Sisters for making sure Maxton's story came full circle, for falling in love with him as much as I am, and allowing me to be vulnerable and face my fear of sharing my first book. Without their magnificent editing skills, you would not be reading this.

Thank you to all the fabulous people behind the scenes that made this book come to life and arrive here: Rachel at Fusion Creative Works for my amazing cover art, Trish for being an author's best friend and sidekick, and Adriel for her formatting genius.

This last one might be a little strange, but I'm not sure if this book would have ever been written if it weren't for the pandemic. I started writing about Max around Memorial Day 2020 not long after Idaho shut down due to Covid-19. With nowhere to go and endless time to binge watch Netflix, I came up with the idea for this book. The majority was written within a few short months and finally completed just over a year later. While I should have been in Italy, I was falling in love with Maxton. And I hope you did too.

ABOUT THE AUTHOR

Lauren Tyler grew up on the pages of *Nancy Drew*, *The Boxcar Children*, and *Anne of Green Gables*, which later gave way to the works of Jane Austen and Ernest Hemingway.

Lauren is an insatiable reader, and the only thing that rivals her love of books is her love of the sun. She loves to explore, both cities and the outdoors alike, and is always up for finding a new favorite haunt. You can find her most days soaking up the rays with a great bottle of wine, a dear friend or two, and her talkative cat Pantouffle. She lives in Boise, Idaho, and this is her first novel. Find her on Goodreads!

facebook.com/laurentylerauthor

instagram.com/blondierocket

goodreads.com/laurenctyler

ALSO BY LAUREN TYLER

Spark: a guide to kickstart or reignite your creativity

To Those Who Came Before

Maxton

Austen

PUBLISHED AS W.B. FORD

(retellings of novels by Max Collier)

Chloe

Leah

Eva

Samantha

Along Came Cathy

CONNECT WITH LAUREN

www.elle-tea.com

Interested in joining our Advanced Reader's Team? Apply today!

Sign up for my newsletter to be the first to know!

Last but not least, all reviews are greatly appreciated! Please share your thoughts on this book (and all the rest) on your favorite reviewing platform.